Murder

at

Yarn Mansion

Yarn Genie Mystery III

CELESTE BENNETT

Island City Publishing LLC

Copyright © 2018 Celeste Bennett
Cover illustration by Christa Scheck
Editor: Katharine Scheck
Published by Island City Publishing LLC
Eaton Rapids, Michigan, USA

ISBN-13: 978-1-946890-06-1
ISBN-10: 1-946890-06-5

DEDICATION

I dedicate this book to yarn lovers everywhere. The ones who have storage cases under their bed, in shoeboxes in their closet, in baskets on the living room floor, in totes stored in the basement, and who have entire spare bedrooms stuffed with yarn. I know you do this because it takes one to know one.

Imogene.

CHAPTER 1

After all I had been through, I had yet to experience a night as dark and as cold as the night I packed to leave my mansion. Laughter and champagne corks popping wafted up to me from the dining room below. If I hadn't been so distraught, I would have found it funny that a knitting agoraphobic like me was more frightened to stay in my home than to leave it.

I stifled a sob, squared my shoulders, and swallowed hard. No one attending the party downstairs was going to see me leave my home in tears. That was because I was going to sneak down the back stairs and go out through the kitchen.

I didn't have a clear destination in mind; I only knew I couldn't stay there.

I pulled all my yarns away from their hiding spots around my bedroom suite: the linen closet, the bathroom, the walk-ins, the purses, and the shopping bags I had secreted behind my winter coats. Once all the yarns were piled on my bed, I got my suitcases out.

The reds, blues, pinks, lavenders, yellows, golds, greens, and every other color of yarns imaginable were spilling over the sides of the bed and onto the floor. There wasn't enough room in my small Chevy to take all my precious yarns with me so I had to decide which ones would make the cut and which ones wouldn't. I picked up a skein of bulky green twist yarn. It screamed winter hat at me but I shushed it and laid it back on the pile. I already had a winter hat. I ran my hands over the six balls of soft angora, but in the end, I ignored its pleading to be made into a sweater and moved on.

The purple strands of chenille I had picked up were starting to get wet. I hate it when I cry over yarn, but I couldn't stand the thought of leaving any of them behind.

The laughter and tinkling glasses from downstairs were getting annoying, so I got up to close my bedroom door only to find my cousin, Mandy, standing there with a glass of champagne in her hand, watching me. Mandy was also my half-sister thanks to an affair my father had with my mother's sister.

Mandy had swept her long, light blond hair up into a mass of green and red colored curling swatches. She had green eye shadow over one eye and red over the other with matching brows. Her golden threaded black dress barely reached mid-thigh. Her upper lip was red. The bottom lip, pursing out in a pout, was painted green.

"I thought you were going to come join the party to celebrate," she said. I watched in fascination as the green and red lips separated and pulled together with each word.

"What do I have to celebrate? The fact that you've moved your lunatic murdering brother into my house?"

"He's not a lunatic; he's not murdered anyone. It's been proven that he didn't attempt to kill you—no matter what you think." She looked over at my bed and raised her one green eyebrow. "This 'yarn mansion' is not just yours now. If you didn't want me to live here, you shouldn't have added my name to the deed."

I grabbed the nearest skein of baby blue sport yarn and fiddled with the strands, avoiding her gaze. "You're my sister. I put your name on the deed because Aunt Tilly wanted us both to share in the inheritance she left. And, I wanted you to live with me so we could make up for lost time. I just didn't realize

2

you'd move Martin in with you."

"You expected me to just leave my brother out in the cold? He's your cousin. He's family. You treat your yarns better than you do him. Insisting he live in the basement is just preposterous. There are plenty of empty bedroom suites in this house. There's even that butler apartment on the third floor that isn't being used."

There wasn't time to get into all the reasons why Aunt Tilly treated her butler so lavishly, so I only said, "Gordon has a life lease on that apartment, and there is nothing legally I can do about it, and I don't want to talk about Gordon, Martin or you. I want you to leave."

"All right. I'll leave your room. It's a mess anyway."

"Not just the room. I'd prefer you leave the house. It would be the decent thing for you to do since you lied in court to get your brother exonerated of attempting to kill me."

"I only spoke the truth. Martin wasn't trying to murder you. You always was a high-strung, nervous little thing who could never take a joke. You got all these phobias that get the better of you."

She was right about the phobias, but her courtroom testimony made it seem like I'd spent my inherited billions on shrinks when in reality the bigamist I'd married was the one who had stolen all my money and then hid it in foreign bank accounts.

Mandy pointed at the suitcase where I'd shoved a few articles of clothing in before I'd gathered the yarns. "Are you planning a holiday vacation?"

"Of a sort," I responded.

"Good for you. You need to go somewhere warm and get some color in your face. You've been way too pale since that FBI creep dumped you."

"He didn't dump me. Frank and I agreed it was better for both of us to go our separate ways."

"Un-huh. If that was so good for you, then why have you been crying and moping around the house ever since you two called it quits?"

3

I shrugged and turned away from her so she couldn't see that her words had upset me to the point of tears.

She wasn't about to give up on me going to her party. She grabbed my arm and tried to pull me towards my closet door. But I'm strong for my size and wouldn't budge, so she let go of my arm and tried a different tactic.

"I'm sorry," she began. "I know you're upset over Martin moving in. I'll try to get him to stay out of your way. Now, go put on that sparkly red knit dress I gave you and come down to the party. I've got a big surrrrprise for you."

I narrowed my eyes at her. I did love the dress she gave me, an early Christmas present. It was angora soft with little sequins embedded in the yarn to catch and reflect the light at every turn. Unlike the skimpy dresses Mandy usually wore, this dress was 3/4 length sleeved with a modest scoop neckline and flowing hem that went down to my knees. I wanted to wear that dress, but not to the Martin-loving party going on downstairs.

"I'm not putting on that dress, and I'm not going downstairs. I will not go downstairs to celebrate Martin's acquittal." I reached out and gave her a slight nudge on her shoulder with my hand. "You're the one who's happy he's off the hook, so you go and have fun."

"Ugh!" She stepped away from me, and some of the contents of her drink spilled out on to my carpet. "You can be so stubborn. The publisher and agent that used to represent Aunt Tilly are down there. They're anxious to talk to you about selling them her unfinished Detective Penelope Pembrook murder mysteries."

"That's the big surrrrprise? I've already told them the unfinished manuscripts are not for sale. Aunt Tilly is dead and to have someone else finish those stories would be fraud and unfair to her fans. Those manuscripts won't ever be finished. I don't want to talk to either of those men. I can't believe you even let them in the door."

"They said you wanted to see them, but they aren't the surprise."

She walked over to my closet, pulled the slinky red knit off the padded hanger and tried to force the dress into my hand. "I don't want to spoil the surprise, so just put the dress on and come downstairs."

"Why do you need me downstairs and in that dress?" I gave her a long, hard look, refusing to take the dress. She was smiling and dancing on the tips of her feet, barely able to contain her excitement.

"Okay. Okay. I'll tell you the surprise. Garrett Edmond is downstairs. He's been calling me a lot, asking about you. He seems real anxious to reconnect with you again, especially since I told him that FBI agent is out of the picture."

When I frowned and clamped my jaw shut tight, she tipped up the drink she'd brought with her and downed it in one gulp.

I picked up one of the balls of yarn from my bed and threw it at her. "You were trying to get me into that dress to impress Garrett?" I threw another ball when she dodged the first. "I can't imagine why he wants to see me, let alone see me in that dress. We didn't exactly part on the best of terms."

Garrett was the secret service agent who arrested me for counterfeiting one-hundred dollar bills when all I'd done was work as a receptionist for the counterfeiters.

"If you like him so well, you wear the dress." This next ball hit her in her ample chest. "We look enough alike that he can pretend you're me."

"I wish." She held up the red knit she was holding. "This dress is two sizes too small for me."

"How did Garrett even know there was a party? Did you invite him here?"

"What of it if I did? He's a catch. I'd jump on him in an instant, exceptin' he only has eyes for you. Ever' time I talk to him, he always steers the conversation to you and how smart you were to figure out what those counterfeiters were up to and how you saved his Treasury job an' all."

"Well, I don't want to see him." I returned the next ball I'd picked up back to the pile, emotionally deflated. "There's really no one I care to see right now." That wasn't entirely true, as a picture of Frank flashed up in my mind to put another twist to the knife protruding from my heart. Figuratively, of course. If I didn't want that knife to keep twisting, I had to focus on something else, or I'd start crying again.

I walked just past Mandy and looked around in the hall. "Where'd you put Mr. Mister for this holiday acquittal party?" I asked. Mr. Mister is Mandy's yippy, obnoxious little white Pomeranian dog. Mr. M sort of grows on you once you get to know him.

"I shut him in the laundry room."

When I growled and advanced towards her, she added, "I left him plenty of treats and gave him some of my tranquilizers to keep him quiet."

"Your tranquilizers! Those are for a full grown adult, two sizes bigger than this dress." I shook the dress she was holding for emphasis. "He's only a little dog. You could kill him if you're not careful."

Mandy reached into the gold lamé purse strapped over her shoulder and pulled out a little bottle of blue pills that she held out to me. "Relax. I cut one of these pills in two. He's fine; he's sleeping. I do wish you'd come down and join the party, even if you don't want to see Garrett. You need to have some fun and loosen up."

I grabbed the bottle of pills, trying to read the label. It was too faded, so I gave up and sat the bottle down on the dresser, hoping she hadn't harmed her little dog.

"Martin's lawyer and all his new friends are here," Mandy told me in her I've-got-a-secret voice. "Martin wants to make things right and have things get back to normal around here."

"Martin's normal is abnormal. I don't want to be anywhere in the vicinity of him or near anyone who would want to be in the vicinity of him."

"Look, he's trying to make amends. He invited reporters. They'll be here in a few minutes. Martin's attorney thought it would be good publicity if you'd join Martin at the party, wish him well, kiss and make up to show there are no hard feelings."

"Ewww." I make a gagging motion with my finger at my mouth. "I do have hard feelings. Martin's high priced attorney can go to hell and take Martin and the reporters with him."

Mandy said a few choice words about my character, flung the red dress down to the floor and stomped on it. "Suit yourself, you baby. I'm glad none of my friends know you're my sister. You can rot up here with your rotten yarns, or you can pack your yarns and leave; I don't care which. I'm not leaving, and neither is Martin, so just get over it."

She left, slamming the door behind her.

I moved some yarns out of the way and sat on my bed trying to control my crying. Everyone I loved had either turned on me or left me. Even Frank had quickly agreed to end our involvement under the pretext of keeping me safe from the dangers of his undercover FBI job. I doubted I'd ever hear from him again.

After a few minutes, I got my crying under control, wiped my eyes with the already wet purple yarn, and started packing again. I folded the navy pinstriped skirt and white blouse I'd borrowed from Janey, Frank's sister, and slid it into a mailing envelope addressed to her new address in Virginia where she'd moved with her husband and baby. Janey never thought Frank and I were suited for each other because he thrived on danger and I was a mouse who ran from my own shadow. Turns out, Frank must have thought she was right.

I picked up the black slinky dress that I once bought to please my bigamist husband, Jorgji. When I bought that dress, I hadn't known he already had a wife that wanted him to kill me to get my billions. He cleared out my bank accounts and hid my money so well even the FBI crime investigation unit couldn't find a single penny of it after his wife murdered him— for not murdering me.

I dropped the black dress to the floor along with the red knit and kicked the red and black mess under the bed. As I pulled out some clothes to take with me, the rose corsage I'd worn to the father-daughter benefit dance tumbled down from a shelf in my closet. I caught it and pressed the dried brittle flowers to my nose to smell any scent of rose that might still linger there. Since my father had presumably died when I was six, my aunt insisted I go to the dance with her butler, Gordon, as my escort.

I gave a harsh laugh as I dropped the withered flowers to the floor and crushed them under my shoe. My aunt was pretty crafty. She'd hid my father right under everyone's noses for years to keep the government from finding him and charging him with treason. It was only recently that the rumor of his still being alive resurfaced and the government reopened their double agent allegations against him. Just before the story broke to the news, the coward fled to Nepal leaving me to fend off American and Russian agents who routinely harassed me for information on his whereabouts. I was too ashamed of him to tell them he had been masquerading for 20 years as my aunt's butler.

After I had rifled through all the clothes in my dressers and closets, I settled on packing only a few T-shirts, jeans, underthings, socks, personal hygiene items, and a bulky cable knit sweater I'd knitted. I zipped the case shut and then turned back to the mountains of yarns on the bed.

Even if no one loved me, I at least still had my comfort yarns. I pulled out my big Gucci carry bag and stuffed it with the worsted weight greens, some of the golds, some of the blues, and as much black and white yarns as I could get my hands on. You could never have too much black or white yarn; they're universal, like type O negative blood.

I left most of the bulkier, common yarns behind on the bed with a gigantic assortment of clothes I hadn't packed and headed down the back stairs to the kitchen. The closer I got to the kitchen the louder and more raucous the laughter in the dining room and the great hall became. I could picture the partygoers gathered around the long dinner table, toasting to Martin's success at fooling the judicial system.

The feel of his fingers squeezing around my neck was still

fresh in my mind. I remembered the panic of losing air, remembered the shock of realizing that I was going to die.

The defense attorney's expert witnesses explained away the bruising found on my neck. The attorney alleged Martin had only 'pretended' to choke me. The expert claimed it was Frank's roughly pulling Martin's fingers off me that caused the bruise marks.

When our father was named public enemy number one, Mandy had begged me to keep her relationship to him a secret, so when asked on the witness stand why I thought Martin wanted to kill me, I refused to tell the jury that Martin wanted me dead so his half-sister could come forward, as the last remaining heir, and claim the family fortune.

I kept my word to Mandy, and Martin walked free.

CHAPTER 2

I probably should have thought through sharing half of my inheritance and my house with Mandy. I should have thought through leaving just weeks before Christmas, too. I was broke; I never liked driving in the dark, and I was too emotionally distraught to be out on the road, but leaving the house seemed the only way to escape my heartaches and the noise of the Russian folk band Mandy had hired.

"Happy Holidays to me," I said as I picked up my Gucci bag, my suitcase, and the diaper bag I used as a purse. I turned out the bedroom lights and headed down to my car I'd parked in the second garage just off the kitchen.

The back staircase was more of an old fire escape route than a staircase. The enclosed steps ran down the back of the house from the third-floor attic down to the ground level, with a direct access into the kitchen, from there I could exit through the back door and out to where I had parked my Malibu—sight unseen by the party goers.

I set my stuff down on the kitchen floor and opened the laundry room door. Mister M jumped up from his spot on my pile of dirty laundry and came over to me, tail wagging.

"Hi, little fella. I just came to make sure you were okay

and tell you good-bye." I checked to make sure he had water in his dish. On the floor nearby, there was a partially dissolved blue pill. I kicked the pill under the dryer, away from Mr. M, and went to the fridge and pulled out a bottle of cold mineral water. As I poured the water into his empty water bowl, Mr. M licked my hand.

A big lump formed in my chest as I rubbed his little, white, furry head and looked into his beady black eyes.

"You be a good dog," I kept repeating to him. I opened my diaper bag purse and pulled out a crocheted goofball I'd made him for Christmas, complete with eyes and teeth and squishy stuffing.

He yipped when he saw the ball in my hand.

"Shhh. You don't want them to come in here and try to give you any more pills do you?"

He sat down, eyed the ball expectantly, and yipped again. I threw the ball onto the laundry pile. He raced to it and brought it back to me.

"I can't stick around to play. I have to get away from here before I lose what's left of my mind. Maybe Mandy will play with you later." Then I thought about how long Mandy usually slept after a long night of partying. "Maybe tomorrow evening she'll feel like playing."

I sat the ball on the pile of my dirty T-shirts, socks, and jeans. Mr. M climbed on the mound, circled around three times, curled himself up, lay down and began chewing on the ball.

Worried about how he would fare with a self-absorbed Mandy after I was gone, I rushed back upstairs and got the pill bottle Mandy had shown me. I brought it down with me and threw it in the kitchen garbage can. Then I buried it under some food wrappers and garbage.

Feeling better about leaving Mr. M behind, I went in and gave him another pat. He wagged his tail into the mound of dirty clothes but was too engrossed in his ball to bother to get up. Glad he liked his gift, I watched him chewing until I had the laundry room door fully closed.

When I got back to the kitchen, Garrett was there. Buff, tan, blond, and still as movie star handsome as ever in his black tuxedo with a red tie and silver vest.

He was gorgeous, witty, charming; fun even. We had gone out once or twice, but the relationship was entirely sparkless where I was concerned. Given what Mandy had told me about his interest in seeing me again, he must have felt otherwise.

Mandy might have invited him believing we were destined to be an item, but we weren't.

"There you are. I was wondering when you were going to make an appearance."

Even from where I was standing I could smell the liquor on Garrett's breath, and his eyes looked a little glassy. His tie and the top button of his shirt were undone. He had a Martini in each hand. A green olive was in one, a small onion in the other, both sunken to the bottom.

I knew the feeling.

"Hello, Garrett." I tried to sound light-hearted and yet brusque, trying to make my appearance in the kitchen seem as natural as possible. Without looking at them, I tried to remember if I had shoved the suitcase and bags close enough to the end of the counter to hide them from his view. I had wanted a quiet exit.

"Is that all you have to say? After all we meant to each other?" He stepped closer, teetering, and slurring his words. Never a good sign.

His mind was the only place where we meant something to each other. "I don't believe we have anything to talk about," I said.

"If your lips don't want to speak to me; then how about a Holiday kiss?" He put one of the glasses on the counter, pulled out a sprig of mistletoe from his pant's pocket and put the sprig behind one ear. He closed his eyes, puckered his lips up and leaned towards me. I took that moment to step away from him to go over and pick up my luggage. He was still puckered and blind when he began swaying a bit. I tried to get past him before he opened his eyes, but all I ended up doing was bumping the glass in his hand.

He jumped. His eyes popped open as the slosh of cold drink penetrated his shirt.

"Shit! You didn't need to do that." He sat the glass down on the counter next to the first, snatched up a tea cloth from the counter and began dabbing at his saturated shirt.

"I'm sorry. I didn't do it on purpose. I'm just not in the mood. Okay? You can get another drink to replace it out at the party. Which is out there." I pointed to the door leading towards the dining room. "On second thought, maybe you could use some coffee." I headed over to where there was usually a pot brewing.

"I don't want coffee. I want you." He started in my direction and grabbed for my arm.

I maneuvered around his staggering body easily and crossed to the other side of the room to get him coffee.

He didn't try to follow me; he headed towards the extra bottles of liquor stored on the counter. Even in his inebriated state, he saw my suitcase, bag, and purse where I had sat them near the door.

"Skipping out on the party? Or going to rendezvous with your boyfriend in whatever gutter he's in tonight?"

"Where I'm going is none of your business."

"What do you see in that bum? What's he got that I don't have?"

The list was too long to begin listing. I looked longingly at my bag and suitcase and wondered how much of a scene it would cause if I just stepped out of the room and out of everyone's lives. I didn't want to hurt Garrett's feelings, but I felt being truthful was the only way to get him to leave me alone.

"I'm sorry you misunderstood my feelings for you, but I don't love you. I'm not even sure I like you, but I do know that I don't like you drunk."

He swayed and his blue eyes turned to ice. "You led me to believe you cared for me. You'll regret that you ever played me for a fool. I know a lot of people in high places."

I went to pick up my things. Garrett stepped in front of my path.

"Please get out of my way. I'd like to leave. I am not going to discuss my actions with you. You're drunk." I tried to step around him, but he shifted to keep in front of me.

"You're going to meet your pugilistic FBI boyfriend, aren't you? Admit it."

"He's not my boyfriend."

"I could call one of my buddies on the police force to tail you and prove you're lying. In fact, I might call them and have them arrest you for stealing my heart. You should really reconsider your feelings for me. I could make you happy." His eyes scrutinized my chest before looking at my face. "Or, I can make your life miserable. The choice is yours. Will it be your boyfriend or me?"

"Threatening me is not going to endear you to me, and I'm not lying. Frank is not my boyfriend. I'm not going to meet up with him, and you can't make my life any more miserable than it already is. Now, I would like for you to get out of my way."

He continued to stare at me like his look alone could change my mind. When he didn't move, I glared back at him and raised my booted foot high, intending to tromp on the toe of his shiny black shoe as hard as I could. Fortunately for him, a woman in a red dress slinked into the kitchen at that moment.

"Where's my drink, Garrett? You've been gone a long time." She looked at the darkened splotch on his wet shirt and the sprig of mistletoe dangling from one ear. She then squinted at me.

I squinted back at her.

Her hair was light brown, cut into a feather cut that framed her triangle shaped face. She was slim and maybe just over five feet tall. The dress was a similar cut and style to the dress Mandy had given me—a lower neckline and much shorter hem notwithstanding.

Looking into that woman's brown eyes, I felt like I was

14

looking into a mirror—if I'd put on a half a ton of makeup and that red dress that Mandy had insisted I wear. This woman looked so much like me I wondered if my father had had another lover other than my mother's sister.

The woman blinked her sparkly midnight blue eyelashes as she sized me up, but I saw no recognition of our resemblance to each other in her face. Just annoyance that Garrett was in the kitchen talking to someone in jeans, ankle boots, and a thick sweatshirt.

"What are you doing in here with the kitchen help? The bartender is out there." She nodded her head towards the main living area.

"Sorry, Lana, darling. After the bartender had fixed our drinks, he ran out of vodka, so I came in here to get him some more. I thought I saw someone I knew in the kitchen, so I stayed to see if it was who I thought it was. Turns out, I was wrong. This is a nobody." He picked up the drink with the olive and handed it to Lana before picking up the almost empty glass with the onion.

"I thought a martini was made with Gin and Vermouth?" Miss Red Dress took a small sip of her drink.

"This bartender prefers vodka. I think he has the right idea. Switching to something different just might be the ticket to a good evening." Garrett turned pointedly towards me, his eyes boring into mine.

Miss Red Dress narrowed her eyes at me again, then gave her attention to Garrett. Dipping her fingers into the glass he was holding, she fished the onion out and sucked it into her mouth with a popping noise. She sloppily licked each finger as she pressed herself up against the length of Garrett's wet front. She began unbuttoning his shirt while kissing his neck. "Honey, you're all wet. Better take those soaked things off. How many bedrooms do you think a mansion like this has?" she asked him.

Garrett's eyes began to close as she licked his exposed skin. "I'd say plenty. Shall we go see if any are unoccupied?"

I fled the house.

CHAPTER 3

An empty feeling threatened to devour me as I sat in my Malibu in the garage. I sat there for a long time just thinking and listening to the muffled din of laughter, the band Mandy had hired playing their strange sounding folk songs, and in the interludes, champagne corks popping. When the band shifted into a loud rendition of "For he's a jolly good fellow," and everyone joined in the chorus, I started my car.

There was nothing for me there. No one was upset that I wasn't there, except maybe Martin's attorney and the press.

I had enough money to hole up in a hotel room for a short while—a very brief while. If I could find another job, one without murderous crooks for bosses, I could afford a small apartment or a room to rent, and I'd never have to come back to this mess, never have to face my troubles.

I looked at the mailing package on the seat next to me wondering if I had enough gas money to get to Virginia and deliver the package to Janey in person.

I hit the garage door remote opener and backed out into the drive weaving my way around the parked cars to get to the main road.

A black sedan parked on the city street at the end of my

driveway pulled away from the curb as I drove past. I got a prickly feeling at the back of my neck. The CIA and Homeland Security had warned me that as long as my public enemy number one double agent father remained at large, I was in danger of being snatched up by Russian agents as ransom bait to flush my father out of hiding and get him to give them the stolen missile plans. The U.S. government had asked me to turn my father in if I heard from him—and I would have, except he'd broken off contact. That left me alone, needing to protect myself from men in black sedans.

I did a U-turn and headed back into the garage, where I closed the door and left the Malibu running as I dashed up the back stairs and into my bedroom. Knowing how easily pretty yarns distract me, I kept my eyes averted to the floor, away from the bed, purposefully avoiding the yarns heaped there.

I detest guns and usually wouldn't have had anything to do with them, but for this occasion, I crawled under the bed and found my dog-chewed slippers where I'd stashed the small Remington pistol Frank had given me for protection. The slippers were empty. I felt around and found the gun was with the dust bunnies that were hiding there. I must have accidentally kicked the pistol when I booted the dresses under the bed.

I felt the heavy weight of the gun in my hand, wondering what I thought I could ever do with it. I didn't even know where to stash it. I didn't have a holster or even a pocket that would hold it.

It stretched out the top band of my hand-knitted socks, but at least the pistol stayed in place when I slid my jeans down over the bulge, so I called it good.

I would have never used that gun, I had only retrieved it for the intimidation factor and because it was a keepsake from Frank. Feeling nostalgic, I thought maybe I should take a few other mementos, too.

I straightened up from the floor and drew in a sharp intake of air when I saw what was on the top of my bed.

My head began to pound. Blood rushed in my ears. The

sights and sounds around me receded as the room started to spin.

I forced myself to look again, disbelieving that what lay nestled into the heap of yarns on my bed was a naked woman with a small bullet hole in the center of her forehead. I averted my eyes when I recognized Garrett laying face down next to her, naked as well.

I didn't want to faint on top of her and I sure as heck wasn't going to faint on top of him, so I plopped down to the floor and put my head down between my outstretched legs.

My God, who would kill two people in my bedroom? And why? Poor Garrett.

My brain flooded with emotion and memory of the time Garrett and I had gone to dinner at the Wells Tower, and all the other times we'd shared. He was so charming. So sweet. At least he had been before I rejected his advances.

I didn't know the woman, Lana, but she hadn't deserved a bullet to her head any more than Garrett deserved to die. When I thought about their last moments together, frolicking naked on my bed, on my yarns, I gagged.

Nostalgia over.

What did all this mean for my departure?

I couldn't wait around for the police. I needed to get out, and get out while getting out was an option. Knowing I wouldn't be able to come back, probably ever, I fished around under my bed and found the box that held my childhood mementos.

The unique stones and trinkets I'd collected from different places, ribbons, the letters my parents wrote me when they went away on business trips, and the dented tin heart from the princess wand they had given me for my sixth birthday. I put the box under my arm and dashed back to the car like a football player scoring a touchdown.

Once behind the wheel of my car, I slammed my vehicle into reverse and left. The band was playing loud enough to wake the dead as I re-pulled out of the garage, wishing that old cliché could somehow have been true.

To avoid the man in the sedan at the front curb, I headed to the drive that wound behind the house to a road in the back.

While coasting out to the back drive with my headlights off, I pulled out my cell and dialed 911.

"I'd like to report a double homicide."

CHAPTER 4

I had only just finished my call, so when a siren scream pierced the night air and a police cruiser pulled up to the house, I was puzzled at their rapid arrival. I figured since they hadn't had time to respond to my call, they were probably responding to a noise complaint from the neighbors. As I continued to exit out the back drive of the house, in my rear view mirror I could see another police cruiser enter the front drive.

I was at the main road, picking up speed, but still leery of the black sedan finding me, so before I turned my headlights back on I checked my mirrors to make sure I was not being followed. That's when I was startled by the flashing police lights coming rapidly behind me. I pulled over to let the police pass and was even more surprised when the cruiser stopped behind my Malibu.

One of the two officers got out and approached my car. Knowing the routine, I nervously fished my driver's license out and handed it to him.

He studied it, and a puzzled look crossed his face. "You're the niece of Matilda Warren, that famous mystery writer that just died a while back, right?"

"Yes, I am." I was amazed that he had made that

connection since my license still had my married name of Dalmat. "Did you read her books?"

"Nah, that Penelope who solved the crimes was a girl; those books were for girls."

Offended, I told him, "I handled all of my aunt's correspondence, and I can tell you many boys and men wrote to tell her they found her mystery books to be a good read." I wanted to brag about how even tough FBI agents liked my aunt's girly books, but that seemed irrelevant to everyone but me.

He squinted at me. "I heard her body was exhumed under the suspicion of murder. That true?"

I had ordered the exhumation under the belief my fraud husband had killed her, but the medical examiner found no evidence of foul play. However, I didn't feel inclined to tell this man who didn't like her books anything about her death, especially given there were two dead bodies back at my mansion, so I said, "No."

I was flat out lying and that caused me to sweat in the cold night air. I put my hands down to rub them on my jeans.

"Keep your hands where I can see them," he shouted.

I immediately jerked my hands back up to a position just beside my face.

"Didn't you just come from the party at the Warren Mansion?" he asked, backing away a bit from the edge of my car.

"Not technically," I stammered, wiping my face with my hands. I tried to calm myself as I felt an anxiety attack begin. "I was never at the party. The party was my cousin's idea. I only live in the mansion." I could feel my heart race. "Or at least I did."

The officer's gun was out of its holster, another not good sign, but he kept it down at his side as he addressed me. When he looked in the back seat and saw where I'd thrown in my trinket box, my bag of yarns and my suitcase, he asked, "Were you planning on going somewhere?"

"Yes. I'm getting away from here."

"Where were you going?" The gun remained in his hand, visible through my car window.

"I don't know. Maybe Virginia."

I started to lower my hands to rub them on my jeans to get the sweat off, but I remembered I had to keep them where he could see them, so I rubbed my face again.

"Any particular reason why you chose just now to leave?" the uniformed man at my window asked me. He gave a hand signal to his partner in the patrol car. I could hear the guy radioing for backup.

A gun and backup? Was I that much of a threat?

Then I realized what a fool I'd been. It was all so clear. He worked for the secret service and said he had connections with the local police.

Was Garrett was making good on his threat to make my life miserable? Was this police stop his idea of getting even?

There hadn't been much blood on the woman and none on Garrett. She could have had one of those pasted on Halloween tattoos on her forehead.

That had to be it. People didn't get killed at holiday parties. The more I thought on it, the more I knew for certain those officers had to be in on an elaborate prank Garrett cooked up to punish me for rejecting him.

I gave a nervous laugh and said to the officer, "Look, I'm sure this is all very amusing, but I'm going to leave now. You can tell your friend Garrett that I was appropriately horrified to think I might be arrested for murder again, but I'm not falling for his shenanigans."

I put the car in gear, only to find the officer's gun now through the window touching my head.

My heart literally stopped for a beat. I fumbled with the gear shifter but managed to get the car into park.

"Step out of the car ma'am. Hands on your head."

"This is taking a joke too far don't you think?" I began, but my words were cut off as the officer wrenched my car door open, and forcibly pulled me out, swung me around, shoved me against the vehicle, kicked my legs apart, and rudely began to pat me down for weapons.

The gun bulging from my sock wasn't hard to find.

I listened to my Miranda rights while face down on the ground, an officer's knee at my back.

"You're arresting me?" I asked in disbelief when he pulled me up, my hands cuffed behind me.

I shifted uncomfortably in the back seat of the police cruiser, handcuffs chafing at my wrists, an all too familiar feeling.

I tried hard to maintain my composure, but when the officer radioed in, "Suspect found fleeing the scene is now in custody," I cried like a blubbering baby all the way back to my house.

At the mansion, Mr. Arrester could have squeezed in alongside any of the six police cruisers or the ambulance already parked on my lawn, but he chose instead to park near the long hearse-like vehicle backed up to my front door. The "coroner" label was plainly visible from my rear seat vantage. Looking away did nothing to quell my nerves.

Mr. Arrester left his partner to watch over me and went to talk to one of the police officers milling around, speaking into his handset. He stopped what he was doing and they both turned in my direction and carried on a not so quiet conversation.

"She had a small caliber pistol hidden on her. Wasn't very cooperative, so I cuffed and Mirandized her."

"Better take her inside and have the Lieutenant deal with her." The officer pointed towards the house using his handset.

I was pulled out of the cruiser just as a member of the press showed up and shouted, "Hey!"

I looked up, and the reporter got a perfect camera shot of me being pulled handcuffed from the back of a black and white with the coroner's vehicle visible behind me. I knew I'd be front-page headlines again. The reporter was told to take a hike by the police but not before he got a few more shots of me being lead inside to the great hall, where it seemed everyone else in the house had been gathered as well.

I looked around, stunned at how many people had been invited to Martin's party. They were all crammed into what, until then, had always appeared to be a large room. Not so large when you had a six-piece band complete with instruments, six catering staff, my sister, her brother, an assortment of guests, and a contingent of police staff in there.

As I gazed around the room, I felt the hair on the back of my neck stand up and a chill run up my spine. I had the strong feeling the source of my discomfort was not the large crowd; my fear of crowds made me a dizzy hyperventilater, not a hair standing, chilled room-spinner like what I was experiencing just then.

I studied the crowd for the source of my distress. The caterers were easily identified by the gold crown imprinted on their black tuxedo vests. All the party guests were formally attired. Even the wait staff dressed in tuxedo pants, and dress shirts. I was immediately self-conscious of my sloppy attire and handcuffs, but my arrest had been a come-as-you-are, and there was nothing I could do about my clothing's contrast to the tuxedos and evening gowns scattered around the room.

The only people not in formal attire, aside from the police and a blonde-haired person whose back was to me, were the band members. The blond man was sitting on one of the Louie the XIX chairs from the dining room. He had a white neoprene gown that covered him from his neck down to his bare ankles. His feet were clothed in elastic paper booties. He was breathing into an oxygen mask as an EMT pumped up a blood pressure cuff strapped around his arm. I staggered when Mr. Gown turned a bit, and I saw enough to recognize Garrett's profile.

Garrett was alive!

Desperate for more good news, I searched the great hall and studied all the faces. I recognized only a few people: Martin, his defense team, Mandy, and the duo seeking the manuscripts from me. The rest were total strangers. Everyone was distracted and hadn't noticed me enter with Mr. Arrester. Everyone except a young, dark-haired man who was leaning

24

casually against the far wall, openly staring at me.

Unfortunately, Lana was nowhere to be seen.

I swayed again at the knowledge the coroner's vehicle was probably there for Lana. The officer who'd brought me in grabbed my arm tighter and led me to a recently vacated chair by a band member. I sensed the young, dark-haired man's gaze stay upon me as I stumbled my way over to the chair. I didn't recognize him, but from his white shirt, black pants and black vest with the crown logo on it, I knew he had to be part of the Royal Catering staff.

Maybe he's just curious as to why I've been arrested when I so obviously have not been at the party.

When a chill rode up and down my spine again, I knew there was more to his interest than just curiosity.

Animosity perhaps, in the way he's studying me?

I glanced away when he didn't. I tried to focus on the other people in the room, but my eyes kept returning to his gaze that stayed steadily fixed on my face. I forced myself to ignore his apparent interest and looked around the very crowded and noisy room. The members of the band and their instruments were situated next to me. Their flaring black pants were tucked into tall black boots, and black boleros covered their white shirts, obviously costumes of their Russian homeland.

Ronald Rosenthal and Gerald Guildenstein, publicist and agent for my deceased aunt were animatedly conversing with Martin and Martin's attorney. Guildenstein had a martini in his hand and from the way he swayed, it wasn't his first.

Mandy was wringing her hands, talking to a tall woman in a floor-length blue evening gown; the woman was patting Mandy's shoulder in a gesture of reassurance. Everyone else stood around or sat in chairs scattered around the hall, chatting and looking as dazed and confused as I felt.

When Mandy spied me, she ditched the woman she was talking to and ran to me. "Thank God you're okay. The police thought it was you on the bed. Then Garrett came to and told them it wasn't, but no one could find you, and I thought...I thought…"

I wanted to put my arms around her to reassure her, but since she hadn't completed her thought I wasn't sure if she was worried that I might have been dead or she was worried because she thought I might have been the killer.

I was glad my hands were cuffed behind my back, so I didn't have to hug her. I told her noncommittally, "It wasn't me."

A woman and a man who were masked and suited in white techy suits with blue rubber gloves and little paper booties—the same style as Garrett's—came in. The man went over to where Mr. Arrester and the suited man with a badge slung on a cord around his neck were standing.

I strained to hear their conversation over the din of the room. I had to try and tune out Mandy's rambling to catch anything.

"We've called in a ballistics expert to examine the wound and try to identify the murder weapon. He's on his way now. You want anyplace else other than the bedroom processed?"

Mr. Badge Necklace was thoughtful for a moment. "Wait 'til we see what they find in the bedroom. There's a boatload of people here. It's going to be hard to process all these people and keep control of the scene."

"Yeah," Mr. Arrester said gazing around the room. "They're squeezed in here like pepperoni on a meat lover's pizza." He turned to the man with the visible badge dangling from his neck. "You gonna keep 'em all here in this room for now?"

Mandy's head bobbed up at his question, and she stopped babbling to me as her head swiveled in Mr. Arrester's direction.

"Yeah. Too many to haul downtown to question and I don't want any evidence destroyed in the rest of the house. Better to keep them confined to one area. Probably will do the initial questioning here at the house as well."

Mandy rushed over to the men and interrupted. "Do you have to keep them all here?" Her eyelashes starting fluttering and her lips began pouting at Mr. Badge Necklace, who was obviously in charge of the scene and calling all the shots.

"We're paying the caterers by the hour and the orchestra goes on overtime if they are here past midnight." She tipped her head a little and made as if to touch his arm but thought better of it and crossed her arms under her breasts, so they pushed up and almost spilled out of her low-cut dress.

He was talking to her chest when he said, "The caterers need to stay since we don't know the method of poisoning of Mr. Edmond. Could be the food. But, I guess since the band is here just for the music, I'd be okay to have one of the rookies take their statements so we can get the band members cleared out before midnight. We'll need to get their names, addresses, and phone numbers though so we can find them again if need be."

"That would be wonderful if the band could leave, captain. What did you say your name was?" Another eyelash batting and more boob hitching up.

"I'm not a captain. I am a Lieutenant, ma'am. Lieutenant Hershiner."

"Well, Lieutenant Hershiner, I'll be sure and put in a good word for you with the police commissioner or whoever it is that runs your department."

She then ran over to Martin who pulled a pencil and paper from a stand and starting collecting names and contact information for the police.

Gildenstein and Rosenthal tagged along with Martin, asking if they could help. Martin shooed them away from him. Dejectedly they returned to where they had been standing.

A gloved, suited, and booted man, black case in hand, dutifully shuffled in and headed directly to Lieutenant Hershiner.

"We've got the room and body processed. We'll be able to remove the body once the ballistics expert is finished. He says it's an unusual wound, small caliber most likely."

I watched the two men walk past me towards the open staircase just outside the hall. I was sure the gun they took off me was small caliber.

I was getting weak. The room swirled and wavered in my field of vision as the realization dawned on me that Lana was still on my bed—dead, and I was the prime suspect.

The chair I was sitting on wobbled as I teetered and almost pitched face forward. The instrument placed on a stand near me clattered to the floor with a metallic pinging sound; probably something inside it broke. A man from the band raced over, picked up the guitar-like thing, and lovingly cradled it in his arms like a baby, cooing to the thing in a foreign language that sounded like Russian.

I apologized profusely to the man.

Garrett looked up at all the commotion. When he saw me, he made as if to remove his oxygen mask, but the attendant quickly resettled it over his mouth and nose.

"You okay, ma'am?" Mr. Arrester came over to ask me as Mandy ran back to my side. She crouched down next to my chair to peer into my face and steady me with a hand on my shoulder.

I couldn't get the room to stay still. "I'm just a little dizzy. This has all been so upsetting."

From across the room, Garrett batted away the helpful attendant, pulled the oxygen mask away from his face, and shouted in my direction, "Oh! Stop acting as if you don't know what's going on. You did this. This is all your fault."

The EMT put the mask back on Garrett's face. At his outburst all the room chatter suddenly stopped and the room grew abruptly silent. Listening.

"What?" I asked, and then, looking around at the watching crowd, I began to realize the difficulty I was in if even Garrett thought I had killed her. "You think I killed Lana?"

Garrett's hand flew up to stretch the mask out from his face again. "You spilled my drink so I would set down the martini I was holding. You knew I always took an onion in my martini. That made it an easy mark to add a tranquilizer to it. Lana and I had just lain down and gotten comfortable in the room we'd chosen to be in. When I kissed her, I felt the room

28

begin to spin, and it wasn't from desire.

"Next thing I know, I hear a pop, and I can't raise my head off the bed. With supreme effort, I managed to get a hold of a phone and call for help before I passed out cold.

"When I lifted my head again, I found Lana lying dead on the bed with a bullet hole in her head.—You won't get away with trying to frame me for her murder."

"Frame YOU!? What about you trying to frame ME!" I shouted, horrified that I was being accused of murder—again. The ambulance attendant forcefully held the mask tight to Garrett's face so I couldn't clearly hear what he said next, but it sounded a lot like "witch."

I stood up to confront his accusations, but as my hands were still cuffed behind me and with the room still spinning, I lost my balance again and bumped a cello on the other side of my chair. Both of us went down. The cello crashed. Mandy chose to help steady me rather than catch the instrument so I stayed upright. My shoulder was throbbing, and I felt terrible that I had probably broken another musical instrument, but again, handcuffs.

A man, perhaps the cello owner, came running over to pick up the heavy instrument. "Bychit," he said in heavily Russian-accented English. He turned to the Lieutenant and told him, "This cello is specially made in Italy, and that mandolin this woman almost crushed is a priceless vintage 8-string from the Russian Soviet of the USSR. We cannot afford to have our instruments broken. I insist my people be allowed to pack up our equipment before this clumsy ox breaks everything we own and bankrupts us."

"All right." Lt. Hershiner turned to one of the uniformed officers near us. "Have the instrument cases examined to make sure there isn't evidence hidden in them and then let the band pack up their stuff and get it out of here, so nothing else gets damaged."

The lieutenant then turned to Mandy and asked her, "Is there somewhere we can set up and start interviewing witnesses?" Mandy looked to me.

"I guess the study would be the logical choice," I said.

"And you are?" Lieutenant Hershiner asked me.

"Imogene Warren. This is my house."

He looked over at Mandy. "I thought you said this was your party?"

"Technically, we both own the house, but I had nothing to do with the party," I responded.

"Oh yeah!" Recognition lit his face. "You're the woman arrested while fleeing the scene of the crime."

"I wasn't fleeing. I was leaving."

The lieutenant ushered me into the study when it was my turn to recount my story for the evening. I confirmed what Garrett had said about our meeting in the kitchen. From there, our stories diverged.

"His story is only true to a point," I told the lieutenant. "I knew from a previous dinner date that we had been on that Garrett took an onion in his martini, but I had no reason to tranquilize him so I could shoot Lana. I'd never even met her before tonight."

My story was interrupted by a uniformed police officer with a medicine bottle in a plastic evidence bag. "Found this bottle of blue pills hidden in the trash in the kitchen. Want the pills tested and the bottle checked for fingerprints?"

Uh oh.

"I think I would like my one phone call now," I told them.

CHAPTER 5

I stood up from the hard cot I'd been sitting on for hours when I heard footsteps and the clank of keys. I ran to the door of the cell and sweet relief flooded through me at the sight of Frank, who was standing alongside the key-clanging officer.

"That was quick," I said to Frank, peering out at him from between the bars of my jail cell.

"I was already in the area."

I wasn't thrilled with his dead-voice tone and the non-committal response, but what had I expected after our promise to stay apart?

The officer told me, as he swung open the door. "We got some paperwork for you to sign before you can go."

"I'm free to go?"

"Yeah, you're free to go, but you're not to leave the Chicago area."

We all three walked in silence down the long jail corridor. My heart beat to a wild staccato just being that close to Frank. He was clean-shaven, and in a dark suit, with a hint of a tangy aftershave. I couldn't place the scent, something like a mixture of lemongrass, mango, and spices. It was an awkward reunion, made all the more uncomfortable by the man jangling the cell door keys, Frank's extreme silence, and the way he kept his gaze straight ahead and kept his distance from me as we plodded along.

"So why am I being released?" I asked the person at the desk who handed me back my purse and other things.

She shrugged. "Don't know."

I signed for the things they took from me upon my arrest. I recovered everything, except for Frank's gun. That, they handed to him. I was puzzled at the alleged murder weapon being given to Frank but said nothing as we left the precinct house.

Frank didn't utter so much as a word to me as we descended the steps. He remained stony-faced and stiff as he opened the passenger door to his Jaguar for me and then crossed over to the driver side and slid in.

I kept swallowing nervously, uncertain of myself, scared of what he'd say if I pushed him to talk to me.

"Don't ask for the truth if you can't handle it," I thought.

When we hit the expressway, Frank revved the engine up to drive faster than the speed limit. He zipped around semis and buses and turned on the car stereo—full blast.

If he wasn't going to talk, I preferred silence. After a minute or two, I got up some gumption and turned the radio off.

"Where are we going?" I asked when I didn't recognize the landscape.

"You'll see." His hands tightened on the wheel.

"Is it close by?"

"Yup." He kept his eyes on the road. I was pleased he was a careful driver, but his lack of emotion was killing me.

"Why aren't you taking me home?"

"You'll find out soon enough." He eased off the gas pedal a little, and the car slowed to a legal speed as we hit the downtown area of Chicago.

After several more long minutes of total silence, I had to know why he was acting so strangely, so I asked, "Are you mad at me?"

"Hell, no." He turned to look at me then. My heart skipped a beat when I saw a smile twitch at the corner of his mouth. "I'm just trying hard to maintain my composure."

"Well, then. It's good to see you, too."

When Frank looked back to the road and said nothing more to me, I turned the radio back on, at a reasonable volume, and settled back into my seat. Dolly Parton's singing kept me company until Waylon Jennings, Willie Nelson, and then Merle Haggard replaced her on the oldies station.

The close-by place turned out to be a motel on the outskirts of Chicago. When Frank swiped a key card for a ground floor room, I started to tremble. This was not where I thought he'd be taking me. Not that I was going to complain. It was the abruptness of it all that unsettled me. I stepped up nervously outside the door he opened. When he motioned for me to enter into a two-room suite, I hesitated.

Frank was acting so frosty. So calculated. So emotionless. Not at all what I'd envisioned for my first time of going to a motel with him. I stood just outside the doorway, reluctant to advance into the room. I wanted him, but not like that.

"I don't understand why you're acting this way. Why have you brought me here and not home?" I bravely asked, "What can we do here that can't be done just as easily at my house?"

He scoffed, and his only response was a broad smile that gave me some measure of comfort that he was the Frank I was in love with, so I stepped inside the room, and let him close the door behind me.

The second that door was latched, Frank pulled me to him, and I was crushed in his embrace. After several long seconds of nothing but the sheer joy of being held tightly against him, he took hold of my shoulders and moved me back so he could look at my face; his eyes gazed steadily into mine.

That gaze was warm and loving, and I drank it in like the emotionally starved woman I was. He smoothed my hair and glided his hand along my cheek. He pulled me to him again, pressing my face to his chest as he hugged me tightly.

Desire and confusion ran through me. When I lifted my

head to ask him why he had been so distant on the ride here, I felt his lips on mine, and I closed my eyes and reveled in the gloriousness of it. The kiss was sweet and long and sent millions of sensations flooding my body and mind—until I heard a throat clearing and a cough behind us and my sensations short-circuited.

Frank pulled away, and I struggled to clear my head of lingering desire so I could see who had coughed.

"How did you get her to come here so quickly?"

My head snapped back to full attention at the immediate recognition of the voice.

Gordon! Or Timothy. Or whatever my father was calling himself then.

"What is he doing here?" I spat out, anger tensing me as I stepped completely away from Frank. Two traitors in one room were two too many for me.

"Oh, I see," said Gordon. "You didn't you tell her she was coming here to meet me. Did you?"

"No. She called me about another matter before I could put in a call to her," Frank told him. "Then I realized that her call for assistance had worked to my advantage." Frank cleared his throat. "I thought it best for you to tell her."

"Tell me what?" I asked them both. Standing away from them but looking directly at my father. "That you're a liar and a cheat in addition to being a double agent? I already know that." I pulled myself up to my full 5 feet and 2 inches and glared at the man standing not too far from me.

Dressed in an old flannel shirt and blue jeans, he looked older than the last time I saw him. Older, worn out and beaten down. There were bags under his eyes and new lines on his face. His hands trembled, and he seemed to have trouble standing upright. He stiffly sat down on the sofa and motioned for me to sit next to him.

I stood where I was.

"Imogene, I see you've already figured out who I am. You always did have good detective skills, just like the heroine in Tilly's mystery novels." A pensive smile turned up the corners of his mouth.

Sickened, I headed for the door.

"Take me home. Now!" I demanded of Frank.

"So, you've found out that I'm wanted by the government of two countries. Aren't you even interested in hearing my side?" my father asked me.

There wasn't anything that he could say that I wanted to listen to. I turned the doorknob and pulled, but before I could get the door open more than a few inches, Frank placed one hand on the top of it and pushed the door shut. With his hand at the top, he was able to hold the door closed against my efforts to leave.

"Genie, hear him out."

I spun around. Furious at Frank for having brought me there without giving me a clue as to what was in store for me.

"Why should I?" I pointed at my father. "I've had Russian agents trying to kidnap me, and the American government has been hounding me to give them his location all because *he* stole those stealth missile plans to sell to Russia so he could be filthy rich. A father is supposed to care about what happens to their child, not abandon them like he did me when I was six and then again when I was twenty-six."

My father's face blanched and his trembling got more noticeable. I lowered my accusing finger, turned and directed my attention towards Frank.

"That's why you need to hear him out," Frank said. When I stood immobile, arms crossed waiting for him to remove his hand from the door. I was determined to leave.

Frank's gaze held mine for a long moment.

Stubbornly, I didn't blink or look away until he said the word, "Please?"

Oh, God help me. I hated it when he said please like that. I always crumbled.

"This had better be good," I said as I sat down in an armchair opposite the sofa.

35

CHAPTER 6

"I wasn't the one who stole the plans," my father began. "I was framed. I worked undercover for the CIA as the vice president of a tool and die company. That cover job allowed me to travel extensively to secure intelligence information with none the wiser.

"As I was finishing my final plans to leave for Nepal for the tool business, it was happenstance that I tore the lining of my briefcase and found the missile blueprints and instructions in there. I had no idea how they got there. As near as I could figure out, the real thief had planted a set of duplicate plans on me while I was at my company office. He must have also arranged for me to have an accident while I was in Nepal so the plans would be found on me and I'd be the one branded a thief and traitor.

"With the theft attributed to me, and me dead—unable to explain or defend myself—that would take the heat off the real double agent, who would then be free to sell the real plans to the highest bidder.

"My car accident happened just as the thief designed it."

Here he paused and closed his eyes for a moment before continuing. "Your mother always went with me when I traveled for the tool company, but I wish I'd never had her accompany me on that trip. Had I known what was in store for us that time..."

I choked back a sob and steeled myself to hear the rest. Out of the corner of my eye, I saw Frank approach me, but he stopped once he got to the side of my chair. He didn't speak or do anything, but his presence was a show of support that I greatly appreciated.

My father continued. "Your mother was the love of my life. She always traveled with me on my trips because we couldn't stand to be apart. She was always eager to help me with my business ventures, kept me company after the long meetings, never realizing the trips I took were a front for my CIA position. She was so sweet, so loving. I wish it had been me that died in that crash."

"Mother didn't know you worked for the CIA?" I asked incredulously.

How could two people be married for years and one keep such a big secret?

"No. That part of my life I kept secret from everyone, even her. It was safer the fewer people that knew. I'm sure she suspected something, given the late nights I put in, but she never questioned me about it. Always the dutiful wife, she was going to attend a small diplomatic dinner with me that night.

"The mountain roads were slick with rain and mud. A vehicle went to pass us and when it forced me off the road at the precise instance the road veered near a cliff...I knew what happened was no accident."

He straightened his posture up and showed no emotion on his face except for the slight tick at the corner of his left eye. "I'm grateful she was killed instantly; grateful she didn't suffer.

"I was in bad shape and so close to death the attending physician ordered me taken directly to the hospital morgue where he thought I'd drawn my last breath. I lay on a cold steel cart in a chilled room for several hours, in and out of consciousness. When an attendant noticed my hand move, he came to investigate. He about flipped out when I tried to speak to him. Fearful my attackers would find me, I managed to make the attendant understand that I had to appear to be dead. For a considerable sum, he switched my identification with a dead homeless man in the morgue, managed to get my passport papers, and notified my sister.

"Your aunt came immediately. After a short time at the morgue attendant's residence, she got me to Italy where I got medical attention. I stayed hidden in a villa there for months while I had several facial reconstructions on my damaged face and recuperated from my injuries.

"It was during my recovery that I learned that the original weapon's blueprints stored at the Pentagon had been destroyed and the inventor dead from a suspicious heart attack. The CIA launched a full-scale investigation and discovered that the Russians had been offered the missile plans for a very high price.

"Without a trial, I was branded a double agent, and since I was believed dead, and was still in a fragile medical state, I couldn't defend myself against the charges."

"Why did they immediately think you were the spy?" I asked. "What proof could they possibly have?"

"My fingerprints were found on several key pieces of evidence at the weapon inventor's residence where he was killed. I didn't ever meet him, and I have no idea of how my fingerprints got in that man's house. I knew I had been framed for both the theft of the stealth missile plans and its inventor's murder, I just didn't know who had done the frame.

"The repair of the extensive damage to my face and jaw made me unrecognizable to anyone who had known me before the accident, so I came home as your aunt's butler, all the while seeking out the identity of the spy who framed me. Because the spy had access to my personal information and fingerprints, I believe the person who stole the plans and committed the murder was an associate of mine, but I never could get evidence to prove who had done it.

"The government records had been wiped clean of the

original blueprints, making the set the double agent and I carried the only ones in existence. I had given the data chip I found in my briefcase to your mother to hide for safekeeping, telling her it was the new marketing plan for a set of tools that the competition was after. I set out intending to get the original set of blueprints back from the thief before they could be sold.

"Did you get them?" A dread bloomed in my stomach. I already knew the answer. It was why Russian agents were after my father.

"I didn't. I don't know what became of them. After the accident, the spy was free to sell his copy of the plans, but something must have gone wrong with the transaction. I kept my identity a secret to everyone but your aunt, but was able to make some contact with my boss at the CIA. He assured me that the sale of the plans never took place, making the plans I gave to your mother the only set. He knew I was innocent and promised to pursue things within the agency and let me know if he discovered anything."

"Your boss knows you're still alive?"

"I had a very clandestine meeting with him. He wasn't allowed to see my face or gather any information on me, but I trusted David Anderson to listen to reason and hear me out. He told me if I wanted my name cleared, I needed to find the real spy and get back the missing plans—without that, he was unable to help me clear my name.

"I've searched and searched, but those plans have never been found. As the years went by, I found I had less and less desire to leave the life I was living and return to the man I once was.

"Then a few months ago the morgue attendant confessed on his deathbed that I survived the crash. The Russian government learned I had survived the crash, and the past came to haunt me again when the Russians came looking for me believing I still had a copy of the missile plans. That's why they are now after you to get to me."

He stood up, went over to the window drawing the

curtain slightly aside to look out. "I have to get this cleared up to get you out of this mess.

"I wasn't aware that David had known all along that I was with your aunt until he got in touch with me to let me know the news of my being alive was about to break. He said he had uncovered some information of who within the agency was the double agent that took the plans, but it wasn't a good idea to talk about such highly classified information on the phone, so we set up a meeting. I went to the meeting place, but he never showed. He suffered a stroke on the way to the meeting.

"I don't dare contact anyone else at the agency for information because I don't know who was implicated in the investigation David had contacted me about."

I sat still, listening, as Frank had wanted me to, absorbed in what my father was saying. Frank placed his hand on my shoulder and gently squeezed. Unlike other times, the warmth of his touch had no effect on me.

Little by little, I began to see why my father hid his identity from me as a child. But, I was now an adult.

"Why didn't you ever tell me who you were?"

"Your aunt told me I should let you know once you matured, but you always seemed so fragile and easily hurt—fearful all the time. I worried about that. Would I be giving you another fear to add to the ones you already had? I couldn't take that chance. And, as Butler and client, we had such a good relationship by the time you matured; I didn't want to change that."

"Okay," I said slowly, recognizing that I did have more than my fair share of phobias. "But why didn't someone tell me that my cousin was my sister? That wouldn't have compromised your hidden identity."

He turned his gaze to me, and I felt I could look right into his soul when he said, "That wasn't something I was proud of." Then a look of horror briefly flitted across his face. "I mean, I'm not proud of having left Amanda's mother standing at the altar to marry her sister."

Then a smile lit his face, "I am proud of Amanda. She was a delight as a child, and when she and her brother came to visit, I savored every moment with her."

I thought back to their every visit and inwardly groaned. I hated those visits. Their gruff ways and mean spirits tortured me. Maybe if I had known Mandy was my sister, things might have been different. I had always wanted a sister.

My father's face darkened. "No one must ever know that Amanda is also my daughter. It is bad enough that you are in danger. If knowledge of her status were known, it would put her at risk as well. It is bad enough that I constantly worry about your safety."

A little tickle of warmth begin to thaw some of the hardness I'd felt since this entire debacle started. "I think your secret is safe there," I reassured him. "I gave Mandy half of the family inheritance without her having to fight for it in court by proving she was your daughter. If she begged *me* not tell anyone she was related to public enemy number one, I doubt that she's been telling anyone."

"Good." When relief washed over his face, I didn't have the heart to tell him that Mandy now lived in the mansion with me, so that put her at some level of risk just from her close proximity to me.

"I am giving you the key to my apartment at the house," Gordon told me pulling a flat rectangle out of his shirt pocket and handing it to me. "That apartment has been built to withstand all methods of attack and is the safest place I know of. I want you to stay there and not go out until I can determine who was behind all this recent rise in espionage."

"If you couldn't find who it was back then, how are you going to find that out now?" I asked, not wanting to be locked in an ivory tower for the rest of my life.

Gordon ran his fingers through his already messy hair, very un-Gordon-like. "I have retraced some of the connections I made earlier, and have a few new tidbits, to warm what once was a cold trail. David is recovering at a rehabilitation center in Battle Creek, Michigan. I have to find a way to retrieve the information he has and add it to what I already know. Then I might be able to build a case to clear my name.

"I just don't dare go to the center he's in for fear of old acquaintances recognizing me if they see me up close, so I'm going to find someone I can trust to get on the inside in the hopes they can learn something from David. Meanwhile, I'll be working all the angles I know of from the other leads I have."

I looked at Frank. "You're good at undercover. Can't you help my father by getting on the inside of this rehab place?"

"I would if I could, but your dad is wanted by the FBI and the CIA. I'm risking my job just by being here and not turning him in. Besides, I have a pretty high profile case I'm assigned to right now that's going to take a few more weeks to wrap up. I can't take time off without someone questioning why."

"I could do it," I said.

"No!" they both said in unison.

That hurt my feelings.

Trying not to let my pouting show, I walked into the bathroom away from both of them while they whispered to each other. I couldn't fully hear from in the bathroom, but I heard enough to know they were talking about me.

Finally, after a long spell of trying to understand what they were saying without them knowing I was listening at the bathroom door wanting to hear what they were saying, I flushed the toilet, ran the water in the sink, and came out.

"Stop talking about me like I'm not here or I'm too stupid to help out."

Frank said, "Genie, we know you aren't stupid, but you have to stay out of this. Remember the Russian guy in the parking garage that was after you?"

Fear gripped my heart, and my legs turned rubbery at the memory. I walked over and plunked back down heavily in the chair, shuddering involuntarily. The thought of what would have happened to me if Frank hadn't been there to keep me safe still haunted my dreams. "Yes."

Frank came to stand in front of the chair where I was sitting. He put his hands on the arms of the chair and leaned down over me, so I was forced to face that piercing gaze. "Why didn't you tell me Homeland Security had warned you that they felt that guy hadn't been working alone and that other Russian agents might come after you?"

I looked away, but he gently turned my head back to face him. I swallowed and tried to explain. "Because I knew you'd try to protect me and I didn't want you to be hurt when it was me they were after. I was so scared something would happen to you because of me."

He pulled me up from the chair and hugged me to him. "You thought you were keeping me safe from the Russian agents and I thought you'd be safe from the dangers of my FBI job if we split up." He gave a bitter laugh at the irony.

"The Gift of the Magi," my father said. "You each sacrificed what you wanted for the sake of the other, a testament to how far you each of you are willing to go to protect the other." He stood up and retrieved his coat from the back of a chair as he told us, "I think you both need some time to talk, alone. Figure out what all this means for your relationship now. I'm going for a cup of coffee. I too have some things to sort out."

"Wait." I ran to him. I was uncertain of just why I was stopping him from leaving until my arms went around him and I hugged him tightly to me for the first time in my adult life. He felt thin and fragile as my arms encircled him.

He hesitated a second and then he put his arms around me, sighed and said, "My dearest Imogene. You must never be seen hugging me. Ever."

He pushed me from him and held me at arm's length when I tried to reach out to him again. "For both our sakes and the sake of your sister, the world must know me only as your former butler. At least, until I can find a way to clear my name and become your father again."

The truth of what he said hit me like a blow to the solar plexus. If seen by the wrong parties, my hug had the power to shred my life and his.

Horrified, I stepped back.

His arms fell away as he released me.

In total fear for his safety, I squared my shoulders, stood up as tall as I could and said, "Of course. As you wish, Gordon."

Just before Gordon closed the door to the hotel suite, he asked Frank, "Before you get too heavily into your reunion, you will talk to her about her safety? Make her see that for her to stay out of sight is the best plan?"

Frank's face took on a serious look. "I'll do my best, sir."

My forehead remained scrunched in thought as I leaned back in the chair to contemplate what Frank had just told me. He and Gordon had made a safety plan that involved my relocation to Gordon's apartment on the third floor of my home. I was to stay there behind lock and key. Gordon would periodically check on me and supply me with food and whatever I needed while he worked to clear his name. Once his name was cleared, and the danger had passed, I would be safe to resume my life.

How could I agree to give up my newfound freedoms?

"So you think that things are that dangerous?" I asked Frank. "After the call from Homeland Security, I made it a point to keep my home security system on, replaced all the locks with stronger ones and I signed up for Taekwondo lessons. If you think it necessary, you could give me your gun back, and I could try carrying that for protection. Besides, by now the Russians must know that I don't have the stealth missile plans and they have to know I don't have any idea where my father is. Well, didn't have any idea where he was until now."

"This safety plan is just the first step. You have to stay hidden until things die down for a bit. It won't be forever." Frank's hands cupped my face, and his thumbs began stroking my cheeks as those blue eyes flecked with brown studied my face. "As much as I would like to, I have a job that demands much of my time, and I can't protect you every second of the day. Gordon has assured me his apartment is as safe as Fort

Knox."

I huffed out a breath, gathering my arguments together.

Frank didn't give me a chance to start. "This is the only way to make sure you don't end up in the hands of the Russians."

"I don't know...," I had begun to assume responsibility for my own safety recently and found I liked it. I felt my control over my destiny was slipping away as I succumbed to Frank's gentle touch.

I studied Frank's face as he studied mine. I needed to find a crack in his defense on this issue. When he put on a pleading look, I felt myself weaken.

"I'm proud of how well you've managed on your own, and don't want to detract from that, but stop and think about the big picture. If anything happened to you, if the Russian's got their hands on you, you know Gordon would give himself up to get you back safe, even though he doesn't have a clue where the missile plans are."

I thought back to all the times that Gordon had been there for me. True, I hadn't realized that he was doing those things as my father, but that didn't diminish his actions. I knew Frank was right. If I were kidnapped or threatened, Gordon would give himself up to save me. I didn't have any way of knowing what the Russian interrogators would do to him in the belief he could provide them with the plans, but I had enough of an idea to know it wouldn't be pretty or humane.

Besides, now that my yarns and bed had been salaciously compromised, I wasn't too eager to go back home to Martin and Mandy, and a pile of bills I couldn't pay. I began to see the logic in staying hidden, but I didn't see how it was a feasible long-term plan.

"Okay, but I can't stay hidden away in the attic forever. I need to find another job. I don't have any money to live on."

"That's the second part of the plan. Gordon has already paid the household bills, stocked the apartment refrigerator and pantry with food, and he bought you some new yarns. He says the internet service for his place is top rate and he has cable. You've enough resources to stay home knitting for quite a while."

Gordon knew me so well.

Or, he thought he did. Once upon a time, I stayed home knitting—never wanting to leave the safety of my home—but that had no appeal for me anymore. Especially if I might be able to help clear my father's name.

I tried not to let on, but already my mind was thinking up ways to discover where that rehabilitation center was, get inside and locate the recovering CIA boss. I was going to find out who the real spy was even if it killed me. I would just have to borrow a page from Gordon's playbook and change my name and appearance. It wouldn't be the first time I'd changed my identity and looks to evade people who were after me.

Gordon and Frank wouldn't have to find out that I wasn't staying in the apartment 24/7; after all, I was supposed to be in hiding and out of sight so I was sure they wouldn't be looking for me to be elsewhere.

"Seems you both have thought of everything to keep me hidden out of sight for a while." I gave Frank a warm and what I hoped was a conciliatory smile. "What about us? Where does all of this leave us?"

He hooked his finger under my chin to tilt my face up. Just before his deep, sizzling hot kiss, he said, "Now that's the third part of the plan."

CHAPTER 7

Frank left me off at my kitchen back door after I sort of promised him I'd go straight up to the third floor. He kept an eye on me until I was safely inside.

Knowing Frank was back in my life had put me in a jovial mood. The fact that both Mandy and Martin were gone from the mansion to the annual Realtor convention downtown only pleased me more. I hadn't wanted to explain to them why I was dropped off by Frank, or why I couldn't stop smiling, or why I was moving into Gordon's apartment; especially since I didn't have a plausible explanation for any of it.

The Realtor conventions were usually just cover for holiday drinking and carousing, so I was pretty sure I had the run of the house until the early morning hours because the drinking and carousing were the only reasons anyone went—anyone except my sister. Mandy always wanted to be noticed for more than just her annual real-estate sales. Now she had newly acquired wealth to flaunt while she flounced around in something short and skin tight.

With Mandy and Martin both gone I had plenty of time, but lots to do and no time to waste. I went directly to the laundry room to say hello to Mr. M.

The ball I had crocheted him and his water and food bowls were there, but he wasn't. He didn't come to me when I wandered through the house calling his name. I squelched my disappointment and went to gather clothing to take with me to Gordon's apartment.

No one had bothered to clean up the damage made to my bedroom by the forensics team. After I'd stepped over countless piles of clothing, shoes, and yarns on the floor, I began to realize that the forensics team had pretty much left the room the way they had found it. Mandy was right. My room was a mess—just like my life.

Thankfully, everything covered in blood had already been removed by the crime scene crew, so I didn't have to deal with that issue as I tried to tidy up my room a bit. I got my laundry hamper from the closet, and one by one dropped in the reds, blues, pink, lavender, yellow, golds, greens, and every color of yarns imaginable from the bed until the hamper began to overflow. There wasn't enough room for it all, so I left the remaining few yarns on the bed and dragged the basket thing into the closet and closed the door. Once that mess was out of sight, things began to look a little neater.

Next, I began picking up my discarded clothing items from the floor. I wasn't very adept at doing laundry, and since the clothes were all relatively clean and appeared free of blood, I folded and drawered, hung and closeted them.

I picked up my little black dress, the last article of clothing from the floor, and found a picture of me in a raincoat underneath it.

I recognized the McClintock office building in the background, but I didn't recall my picture ever being taken when I worked in downtown Chicago for the counterfeiters. I knew I hadn't brought that picture into my room.

If I didn't bring it, then who had?

Since I was sure that picture hadn't been there before the party, I concluded Garrett had it with him when he entered my room with Lana, where it must have fallen out of his pocket when he disrobed.

After his insistence that I kiss him in the kitchen, his declaring his intentions towards me, and his anger when I rejected him, it didn't surprise me that he had taken my picture without my knowledge. But it gave me the creeps to think he was so obsessed he had to carry my photo around with him. Even creepier was that he'd taken a woman who looked like me up to my bedroom while carrying my picture in his pocket.

I was confident I didn't love Garrett, and I didn't want to deal with the implications of what his feelings were for me, so I threw that picture in the emptied trashcan, whose contents had been sealed away in an evidence bag somewhere, awaiting a trial. A trial that I hoped I would have no part in. The district attorney may have dropped the murder charges against me, but I had no doubt they still considered me a suspect.

Having straightened my room up, sort of, I packed up some of my clothes and headed up to Gordon's bachelor pad.

CHAPTER 8

I sat my suitcase down just outside of the third-floor apartment door. Ignoring the keyhole slot in the doorknob plate, I held the strange little square metal box Gordon had given me to the decorative area below his apartment's doorbell. Once I was sure I had the box squarely centered, I pushed the red button on its side and felt something shoot out and enter the plate just to below the door buzzer. I turned the square box 180 degrees as I had been instructed and pressed the green doorbell button. I heard the lock release. The traditional doorknob and key lock in the door was a ruse designed to fool. Something Gordon was good at.

I didn't know what to expect when I opened the door; I was never allowed inside Gordon's apartment. To my knowledge no one was, not even the maids.

The small foyer inside was just big enough to hold an umbrella stand, a hat and coat rack, and a tray for boots and shoes. I stepped inside, dragged my clothing box in with me, and there I met another doorway.

It was more of an open arch, but I knew from Gordon's description there were laser light beams that intersected the opening at all levels. They might have been visible had the light been off, but it wasn't, because the foyer light came on the second the outer door had been opened. I found the switch for that light and turned it off. In the gloom, I saw immediately that the laser beams crisscrossed enough space to prevent even a dog as small as Mr. M from getting through undetected. I counted down six rays from the top and then over three, drew in a deep breath and said a prayer for the hand I cautiously stuck in the beam in that exact spot. With my left hand, I simultaneously picked up the red umbrella from the stand next to the arch. To my relief, my hand piercing the beam stayed intact as all the beams vanished.

Fearful of the laser light's imminent return, I grabbed my stuff and rushed through the archway. I found the second light switch that illuminated the next room and flipped that on.

The room was small but cozily decorated, with a love seat, small coffee table, two overstuffed chairs, and a desk with a laptop computer. The desk was flanked by broad bookcases. Some of the bookcase shelves held family type pictures of people I didn't know, but the majority of them were stuffed to brimming with books. The entire room was probably no bigger than 10 feet wide by 12 feet deep. There was a small kitchenette off to the side. I opened the first door to the right of that and found the bathroom, complete with a skylight, a garden tub, double sink, cabinet, and a small shower. Much more decadent than the living area of the apartment would indicate.

The door to the left of the kitchen opened into a room with a full double bed, a dresser with a mirror and there at the far side of the room was the most enormous entertainment center I'd ever seen. A large television screen sat smack dab in the center surrounded by lots of drawers, cubbyholes, and shelves filled with high-tech entertainment type electrical stuff.

I had no idea that Gordon was such a media nut.

I went over to the lone dormer window in his bedroom and looked out, but when I realized how far down the ground was I closed and locked the shutters. This apartment had two dormers, one in the bedroom and one in the kitchen. Both faced the front of the house. I shuttered both to keep my acrophobia in check.

The whole place, all four rooms, was tiny compared to the rest of the house, but I didn't mind since I was not going to be staying there much anyway.

I saw bags of my new yarns purchased by Gordon had already been delivered to the bedroom, just as he had promised. They were bright, and colorful, and I ignored them. I didn't bother taking the time to unpack my clothes or things either. I headed straight to the computer on the desk in the living room. I had asked Gordon for the password under the guise of wanting to watch YouTube crochet and knitting videos, but I didn't have time for that. I needed to find the center Gordon said his old boss was in. I knew the bosses' name and since Gordon had mentioned Battle Creek, Michigan, that was where I started my search.

Fortunately, there was only one rehab listed for Battle Creek, and it took only one click to get to the Roosevelt Rehabilitation and Convalescence Center's web address. The header picture at the website was a sprawling white front porch that ran the entire length of a two-story white building. The image captured the sign at the front proclaiming rest, relaxation, and recovery. The porch was dotted with white wrought iron chairs and tables with potted begonias centered on them. You could almost feel the summer breeze ruffling the hair of patrons dressed in cool, thin, white gauzy clothing, straw hats atop their heads while they sipped iced glasses of lemonade and talked about the weather.

I perused the site's header tabs with no luck; I didn't want to know the center's history, their work, or their strategic plan. At the footer area, I found a link for "employment opportunities."

"Well today's my lucky day," I told myself when I read that the center was providing free lodging to anyone with a nursing degree, a physical therapy degree, or nurse's aide certification who would agree to work at their place of employment for at least six full months before seeking employment elsewhere. A company would have to be desperate for help to entice workers with free lodging.

Desperate I understood. Desperate would be my way in.

I looked up what all one had to do to become a nurse or physical therapist. I didn't have time or money to get a degree, so I looked up what was required to be a nurses' aide.

From what I read, it seemed to me that nurse's aide was just a fancy title for some who made beds, emptied bedpans, fed people meals, took their temperature, and helped them take their showers. I wasn't all that keen on the shower part, but if I could remember what I'd read about how to take vital signs, the rest of it seemed like taking care of a baby—only with bigger babies. I'd already done that babysitting thing once with Janey's baby, so that aide job sounded the easiest of my employment possibilities at the center.

I just needed to be sure and carry my cell at all times to keep in contact with Gordon and Frank, so they didn't suspect I wasn't in the apartment and come looking for me.

I got in Penelope Pembrook detective extraordinaire mode and decided to change my persona to go undercover at the rehab facility. Mandy and I were about the same clothing size, give or take about 15 pounds, so I went to see what I could borrow from her wardrobe before she got home from the convention. It wasn't really stealing from her since I would bring them back.

She had lots of jeans with rhinestones, dresses with low cleavage advertisement, and tight skirts that advertised something else. Not the persona I was hoping to achieve but it was definitely not me, so I grabbed up some of her recent purchases of slacks and blouses to take with me. I left the cleavage dangers and tight skirts—they didn't seem very nurse's aide-ish anyway.

In her bathroom, I found bottles of the red and green dye that she had used to get her hair tinted for Martin's acquittal party. I debated on taking the green but left it behind in favor of the red. I didn't want to be an undercover clown, just incognito.

Then I thought about the clothing I had gathered up. They all seemed as clownish as the green and red dye, so I sat them all down on Mandy's bed and went downstairs to see if our former maid, Mary, had left any of her clothes in the small bedroom off the kitchen, where she sometimes stayed when the weather was too nasty for her to go home at night.

The bed, dresser, and small nightstand were still there squeezed in the small room that was once a pantry before the house was renovated. I pulled out the dresser drawers and found only a few underthings and some sleeping attire. It seems demure little Mary liked black teddies and bright red, lacy thongs.

Before I could go examine the nightstand, I heard the kitchen's rear door open. The sound of footsteps was followed by the refrigerator door opening.

I recognized Martin's and Mandy's voices; they'd not stayed the full length of the conference. There, trapped in Mary's room, I couldn't help but hear their conversation while I waited for them to clear out of the kitchen so I could sneak back upstairs.

"We just got through gorging ourselves on caviar and Champaigne. What are you getting into the refrigerator for?" asked Martin.

"I need to get Mr. Mister a bottle of cold water. I can't believe they didn't stock something suitable for him to drink."

I squinted through the slight crack in the door opening out into the kitchen. Mandy had Mr. M in her arms as she searched the refrigerator trying to find the expensive designer water bottles she always kept in there for her dog. He was licking Mandy's face.

"Don't let that dumb dog lick your face," Martin told Mandy.

"He's giving me kisses. He's very affectionate. Aren't you boy?" She snuggled him closer to her face.

"Yeah. Right. If he hadn't have been so affectionate with

Mrs. Silverman's ankle, we wouldn't have been kicked out of the conference center. And, I'd still be sipping Champaigne with Carmelita, who I was just getting acquainted with. I had high hopes for some affection myself. He's your dog, so I don't understand why I had to leave because your dog got amorous with the legs of the conference attendees."

"You are not a realtor. You were there as my guest. If I had to leave, it's only fair that you had to go, too."

"Nothing fair about it. You only wanted to show off your expensive clothes, car, and dog to your work friends; rub their noses in it. Your recently acquitted brother was just along to complete the show."

Mandy sighed. "I had wanted to take Imogene so I could show her off to my friends. Let everyone see how I'm friends with Miss Murder Suspect, but I didn't know how soon she'd be out of jail, so I gave the conference chairman your name as my guest instead."

"Too bad you don't want anyone to know your daddy's a traitor. Makes it so you can't let anyone know Imogene is your sister either. If you could tell them, that'd blow their minds."

"Well, when she called me to say the charges against her were dropped, I told her she should go on that vacation she was going on when she got arrested."

"She was going on a vacation while we rotted in this old house?"

I resisted the urge to pop open the door and give Martin a piece of my mind, but I was enjoying his complaining too much to interrupt him.

He continued on, "I'd go on vacation, too, if we could ever get your stingy sister to cough up those gold-mine manuscripts your aunt was writing when she died."

"Have you been talking to those two pests again?"

At least Mandy could see Rosenthal and Guildenstien for what they were.

"They aren't pests, the one is a literary agent, the other a publicity hound or something, and they've promised me a bunch of money if I can get my hands on those manuscript things."

I twirled my USB bracelet around and checked to make sure the snap part was securely closed and the seam invisible.

"What do you need money for? I got a bushel of it from Imogene. She's still feeling guilty that I didn't ever get to see my daddy much before he died, so I figure that's good for at least another mil before she's broke."

"That'd be your money. I'd like to make me some money of my own. I don't like how you always make me come to you and beg."

"How is selling something that someone else wrote making you your own money? Seems to me that's still money coming from Imogene."

"It'd be money given directly to me, so that would make it my money. That's not the same as the money you get from your cash cow."

I backed away from the door and sat on the small bed in Mary's old room, waiting for them to get the heck out of my kitchen.

Unbeknownst to Mandy and her parasite brother, their cash cow had already been milked dry.

CHAPTER 9

I drove to Michigan and parked my car at the Kalamazoo airport—all the better to hide from anyone trying to track me: Russian agents or angry boyfriends or fathers. The cabbie I called for the remainder of the drive was short and stocky, a jaunty cap pulled down low over his brow, but he seemed competent enough as he cruised down I-94. After several miles, he took an exit, and after whizzing past dead grass, evergreens, leafless trees, and chain link fencing, he turned on a paved road and drove through a pair of open, rusted iron gates. When he began swerving to miss potholes, I sat up and took careful notice of the winding drive we were traveling on.

I lost track of the number of twists and turns as we dogged along. Finally, we came to a weathered white sign declaring the place we were at to be the "Roosevelt Rehabilitation and Convalescence Center." Or more specifically, "Roose it habilitat and Con iescence enter," since several of the letters had either partially or completely peeled away from the weathered wooden sign.

"They certainly have a long driveway," I remarked to the cabbie as he steered over road bumps to the front door.

"Yeah," he told me. "This place used to be part of Fort Custer. Biggest Army training center in the states. I was once stationed here as a new recruit. This section was once a villa for the visiting families to stay at when they came to see the soldiers. Sure is pretty, ain't it?"

I looked around at the bare trees, empty flowerbeds, dirt patches mingled in with brown grass, and the sagging pines, and said, "I guess so."

"Well, it hasn't been a villa for a long time. It might not look like much right now, but you should have seen it in the spring. Course, the place doesn't keep up the flower beds anymore, and I've heard the back section's roof is starting to cave in, but it's a beautiful place when the trees fill out in the spring."

He stopped at the front of a long, gangly front porch and put the taxi in park. While he got my suitcase out from the trunk, I gazed in wonder—wondering if this was even the same place I'd researched. The picture on the website, with its spotless coat of paint and fresh exterior, must have been decades old, back when the place was newly built. Now everything was a flaking and dingy white, the tables and chairs rusty, splashed with mud. The broken pieces of pottery littering the porch were just a sad reminder of the flowers that must have once graced them.

I paid the driver. He took my two bags up the steps and put them just inside the door. I followed him reluctantly.

The enormous foyer was more of a living area dotted with a few threadbare stuffed sofas and chairs. In one corner was a scraggly artificial Christmas tree dotted sparsely with colored Styrofoam bulbs and tinsel. Otherwise, the area was devoid of life.

I tried to envision this huge room as it had been back in its youth. With the high ceiling, gracefully curving oak arches and once beautiful carpet, it was easy to see the grandeur the place had once claimed when families and soldiers frequented it. Soldiers who had not wanted to be forgotten if they perished on the battlefield—judging by the names carved with deep grooves into the scuffed accent tables.

Upon setting down my luggage, the cabbie pulled out a handkerchief and wiped his brow. He looked around the place and must have seen something different from what I'd seen because he said, "Sure is creepy how lonely and vacant the place is now."

He turned to leave me alone in the vast emptiness, and I almost called him back to take me to my car. The knowledge that somewhere in this dilapidated building was a man who might be able to help Gordon stopped me.

I found a service bell on a wide desktop and pinged it. It didn't sound very loud; the sound was swallowed up in the vastness of the room. When no one came, I dinged the bell again.

A Latino woman with a mop shuffled up to me. I asked her where I might find Mrs. Mulgrew, the center's director who did the hiring.

"No hablo Ingles," she said. "Ven aca." She motioned for me to follow her down the hall where she opened a door and ushered me and my baggage into an office area.

As she backed away, a stylish woman behind the massive, ornate office desk put away the papers she had been working on and rose to greet me.

The woman, who I guessed was Mrs. Mulgrew, didn't smile, but she seemed pleasant enough as she explained, in an advertisement style recitation, "The Roosevelt Center was originally built to be a resort. It was remodeled to a state-of-the-art self-sufficient hospital when the base needed a comfortable place to house and care for ill soldiers during World War II. When the T.B. epidemic was under control, the hospital was no longer needed, so the villa was remodeled into a rehabilitation center." She tugged on the bottom edges of her form fitting, shimmering suit jacket and smoothed down the few front creases that had formed in her skirt from sitting.

Almost as an afterthought, she smiled at me and took the papers I handed to her. "We here at the Roosevelt Rehabilitation and Convalescence Center want to continue that long history of comforting families and helping people recover from trauma by hiring only the best in caregivers."

I didn't consider myself the best at anything and I wasn't too confident my desktop publishing program nurses' aide certificate counterfeiting skills had been up to snuff, so I waited expectantly for the worse.

When I had called the center a few days prior, Mrs. Mulgrew seemed pleased with the phony nurse's aide credentials I'd faxed her. She had given me a tentative starting date and instructions to show up with my paperwork and credentials for an on-site interview to complete the hiring process. Now that she had the document I'd forged to examine up close, I looked guiltily down at my suitcase and wondered if I would have any trouble getting the cabbie to come back and get me.

Mrs. Mulgrew tugged at the edge of the jacket to her two-piece suit again, and picked a piece of lint off the cuff. She looked me up and down, and never once glanced at the papers I had handed her.

My cheeks burned as I realized the outfit I was wearing was missing a button on the sweater and the creases in my dress slacks had not been pressed. I didn't know how to use the iron, and couldn't sew on a button if my life depended on it. Fortunately, she made no comments about my disheveled attire, and asked me no questions before she told me I was hired.

I was shocked at her acceptance of my phony aide certificate and relieved that she hadn't asked to see my made-up social security card, too.

Mrs. Janet Mulgrew signed her name below mine on what she called a "letter of commitment" and then she said,

"Welcome aboard, Miss Warren."

Flustered, I didn't know if women shook hands to seal deals or not. When she didn't offer me her hand, I felt relieved. I told her, "You can call me Regina, or my friends just call me Genie."

I had thought it best to keep my last name. It was nondescript, would be less complicated for me, and easier to not slip up with. I chose the first name of Regina, not because I felt it fit me, but because that would make my nickname "Genie", the nickname Frank liked to call me and a name I would be inclined to answer to if taken unaware.

Pleased with my signature, she filed the paper away in a filing cabinet along the wall. The plain-faced, 30-something Mrs. Mulgrew told me I could keep my luggage in her office until I had settled into the staff boarding area. I sat my suitcase down as instructed and followed her to the nurses' station where she introduced me to Dianna, a nurse with dark circles under her eyes and an enormous baby-belly that stuck out in front.

Dianna took me on a tour. We walked down the hall to the left of the nurses' station, and Dianna told me, "This is the East Wing. Most of the residents here are easy to care for. Since you're new, you'll be working days for training. Everyone first starts out on days to get used to the patients, and then we switch them to nights until they get enough seniority to bid on a day job."

We stopped at the first patient room, 101E.

"This is the room for Mrs. Jillian Jones. She uses a wheelchair. Staff get her up, dressed, and into her wheelchair and keep an eye on her to make sure she doesn't forget to go to lunch, dinner, and craft time. Her family refuses to let us put her in adult diapers so she needs to be encouraged to use the bathroom every three hours during the day and gotten up to commode chair every three hours at night or she wets her bed."

I peeked in through the partially open door at a white haired woman sitting up in a chair reading a book by the light of the only window in the room. There was a hospital bed with a bedside table on one side and a metal and plastic chair with a toilet seat lid pulled up close to its other side.

Potty-chair, lunch, dinner, and craft time. Okay. I can handle that.

Dianna coughed a bit and gave a gentle knock at the next door before opening it. A woman lay asleep on top of the bedspread with a stuffed toy dog enfolded in her arms. Her white hair was fanned out over the pillow and her pale, creased face took on an angelic quality in sleep. Dianna pressed her index finger to her lips and quietly guided the door closed.

"That's Zina Flowers," she told me in the hallway. "She has a neurosis that keeps her up most nights. All the patients aren't supposed to go back to sleep once they've gotten up, but Zina lies down. She stays on top of her fully made bed so no one will know that she's gone back to sleep during the day. She isn't harming anyone and I figure at 82-years old she can sleep if she wants. I'm sure it's her valium that makes her sleepy, but we have trouble with her having anxiety attacks if she doesn't take her valium, so I usually just let her sleep. It's easier than dealing with her anxieties."

I'd never taken valium, but the anxiety part of Zina's life I understood only too well.

We moved on to the outside of the next door. I noticed my guide hadn't bothered to open it so we could see inside.

"Mr. George, the resident in this room is an ornery, bitter man who will slap at you if you get within striking distance. Fortunately, he is pretty independent so you won't need to get too close to him. Just check to make sure he showers and shaves every day and is at his table in the dining room for meal times."

Shower and shave from a safe distance. Visual check of

the table. No problem. I can handle that.

I wondered what had made him so bitter—and if he was independent, why did he need to be there?—but didn't have time to ask as Dianna was already moving on to the next room.

That resident's door opened before we reached it. A thin, black haired man peered out. A leer lit his face when he saw us.

Dianna shooed him back inside and closed the door. "Mr. Jake is a dirty old man, so if he asks you to help button his shirt or zip up his pants just decline. He's only here because his family refuses to let him live with any of them and his doctor feels he shouldn't be living alone."

"His physician prescribed a convalescing home for him?" I asked.

"No. His psychiatrist did."

Can I handle that?

Dianna continued down the East Wing, advising me of each patient's names and needs.

Doris had dementia and was always shouting to her brother Andrew—who was in the room next to hers, minus the dementia.

Korry, a teenaged accident victim, had two broken legs, one broken arm, and a broken jaw. He was there for pain management and physical therapy so he could heal and get strong enough to be managed at home.

After that, I began to lose track of the names and situations of the other people tragically placed there either to recuperate or to await death.

Dianna smiled a big smile when we got to the next to last door. "This is Mazie McGuire's room. She's a character. She's only here because her upstairs apartment got to be too much for her bum hip to handle. I'd introduce you, but she's not here right now. She has herself signed out for the morning. I expect her back this afternoon. She sometimes signs out so she can take a cab to visit with her sister in town. She doesn't require any special care. Just deliver her breakfast in the morning, make her bed, and give her fresh water every day."

"Needs breakfast, bed made, and fresh water. Got it." I told Dianna.

Dianna smiled a wider smile. "Mazie is..." She tried to hide her amusement, but it showed in her eyes. "Mazie is...Mazie. You'll like her. We all do. She might ask for extra favors and we always try to accommodate her. Her nephew is part owner of this place."

Special treatment. Check.

The last door of the wing was near a fire exit door. I noticed that the patient's door was closed with a 'no admittance' sign. I'd been given no instructions or introductions for that room.

"Who's in here?" I asked motioning to the closed door with its exclusionary sign.

Dianna paused, put one hand to her back while she rubbed her bulging stomach with the other and said, "This room is not part of your assignment. Mr. Anderson is a stroke patient that needs plenty of rest and quiet. You're not to bother him. His employer pays for a nurse assigned exclusively to him. The only thing the center does is provide him with meals and physical therapy. Or we did when we had a therapist."

My ears perked up when she mentioned the stroke victim's name was Anderson. He had to be the man I was supposed to be getting information from. If I wasn't to bother him, then I had no idea of how I was to accomplish that. I stared at the closed door. No locks, just a push door latch so maybe I could sneak in sometime when no one was looking and his nurse was taking a break.

Dianna next turned a corner and stopped just outside of a door marked "supply closet." She didn't seem to notice that when she opened the door I backed away and started rubbing my sweating palms on the sides of my thighs.

Enclosed spaces are one of my biggest fears, and for good reason.

The rolling racks of linens inside the closet looked harmless enough to most people, but not to me. I was relieved when Dianna didn't step inside—or make me do it. All she did was say, "Here's where you get everything you need to make up the resident's beds, and the towels and washcloths for their baths and showers. Are you going to be staying on the premises?"

"That was part of the employment offer." I took a step back from the open door, and then, thinking I was being foolish, I stepped forward again.

She did a frown and the lines around her eyes deepened. Her face took on a haggard look when she said, "I guess that was bound to happen. They give you a bedding set to start out with. I suggest if you need anything additional, don't ask anyone for it; just come and get it from this closet here so they don't charge your account for another set."

She closed the door. My claustrophobic crisis averted.

"I'm the only nurse on duty right now, so I have to stay in the resident areas of the center, but I'll have someone show you where you'll be sleeping tonight. You'll need to back here at the nurse's station to report in at 8 am. You'll get an update on each patient during morning report in the conference room and then you'll go get your assigned people up just before 9 am breakfast. Your work shift ends at 8 pm so you'll need to get your charges ready for bedtime before that.

"Breakfast is served in the patients' rooms, after that everyone has their bath or shower and daily grooming. Lunch is served in the dining hall at 12:30 pm. Unlike the West Wing where all the patients are tube fed, all the patients from this wing eat lunch together. After lunch, they have crafts or a special activity that most of the residents are required to attend. While they are at craft time, staff put fresh water in the bedside pitchers, make their beds, and freshen their rooms while they are out doing whatever craft activity Pricilla has planned for craft time."

Dianna then muttered something under her breath that sounded like, "Or what Prissy passes off as a craft."

"Excuse me?" I said.

"Oh, it's nothing. I know craft time is just a way to get the residents out of their rooms for a while so they have a chance to socialize, get a change of scenery, and so the rooms can be freshened up, but it bugs me that Pricilla, who doesn't seem to know the first thing about crafting, was hired to do crafts. One month she had them all doing up silly little candy buttons with colored sugar powders. They got the powder all over them. It was such a sticky mess that some of the residents had to have an additional shower to get them cleaned up. It made for a lot of extra work for the staff."

"I certainly hope they will be doing a different craft this week," I remarked, not wanting to assist anyone with their regular shower, let alone do an additional one.

Our last stop of the wing was a wide, spacious room with parallel bars, stairs and ramps, crutches, braces, weights and pulleys, padded tables—all scattered around a huge, green walled room. Most of the equipment displayed chipped paint and some had obvious rust. All except a large, shiny, stainless steel vat that stood off to one side with mist curling up from the water inside.

"We have a few residents who are supposed to go here for physical therapy a couple of times a week. The last therapist left suddenly. He was a goof off who never wanted to work at getting the residents better so I say good riddance. If Grew ever hires a new therapist, you'll bring any of your residents scheduled for P.T. here."

"Grew?" I asked, not understanding the reference.

"Sorry. Mrs. Mulgrew. The staff all call her Grew—just not to her face."

I took a quick look around the therapy room before we

returned to the hall.

I found it odd that Dianna turned to leave this area without telling me about the unpainted wooden wall with makeshift door with a sturdy hasp and padlock at its center.

"What does that area go to?" I asked, pointing at the door.

"That hallway leads to the old lab and x-ray. It isn't used anymore because the ceiling for that section is caving in. The door was boarded up because it is a hazard to go in that area."

I looked at the sealed hallway and my brain whispered "déjà vu" at the "Keep Out" sign plastered to the face of the door.

CHAPTER 10

After that brief introduction to my East Wing duties, Dianna took me to the West Wing, where a few Latino staff in brown uniforms were coming in and out of the residents' rooms. None of them looked at us. None of them spoke to us. No one smiled. Most just kept their eyes averted to the floor as we passed them. Being shy of strangers myself, I understood their desire to avoid unnecessary contact.

The West Wing had a nurses' station, flipped but identical in structure to the East Wing. That was where this wing's resemblance to the East Wing ended.

The hallway in this section was painted tan. The faded photographs of soldiers in military scenes had been screwed into the walls, no attempt to hide the screw heads that stuck out from the metal frames.

I stopped to keep from bumping into a woman coming out of the closest room with a washbasin and towels in her hands. I guess she must have been eighteen to be employed, but she was small and thin, more like fifteen. She looked up as we nearly collided. The water in the basin sloshed. When she saw me looking at her she averted her eyes to the floor and scurried back into the room she'd just come out of.

Dianna looked like she was about to say something about what just happened when she had a pain that stopped her dead in her tracks.

"Braxton Hicks contractions," she explained, panting. "They come and go. They're just to get you ready for the real labor, but I need to stop walking and rest for a brief spell."

We made it to the nurses' desk. An imposing, muscular man with hair so black it had to be dyed was at the desk. No one else was there. He looked up when Dianna and I approached.

"Hello, Dianna." He stood up to greet us, and I saw his sitting height was deceiving as he was only an inch or two above me. Seeing Dianna's distress, he helped her to a chair at the desk. He turned and smiled a brief smile at me.

A smile that never touched his eyes to thaw the cold that I could see resided there.

"Hello, Mark," Dianna panted. "Just a new East Wing employee tour. We'll be as quick as possible, but I need to sit for a minute." Dianna held her stomach as she bent forward.

"Very well." He sat back down in front of a monitor at the desk that showed the interior of several of the patient's rooms. The black and white images on the screen were of hospital rooms with people laying on beds, a few showed the aides moving around the rooms doing tasks. I could see the young girl I'd seen in the hall standing in the room with her ear pressed against the door as though listening. She was still holding the basin she'd been carrying when we last saw her. Strangely, she was just standing at the door, frozen in time.

After a few minutes rest, Dianna seemed recovered, and we moved back into the hallway where Dianna showed me the first fire exit door. It had an alarm bar on it; I presumed all the doors in the residential areas had alarms so staff would know when a patient or resident left the building, but the alarm on this door was different from the ones on the East Wing. This door had a digital keypad in addition to an alarm system.

When I asked for the names of the residents in that wing, Dianna told me, "You don't need to know their names. This section of the hospital is staffed mainly by the immigrants with head nurse Mark Staylee—the man at the desk—overseeing it. The only contact you'll have with this area is if there is a severe staff shortage. Then you might be called on to work in the West Wing, but that hasn't happened in a long time. Not since Grew gave Mark full control of the operation and staffing of this wing. He's very strict with his staff, in ways I don't approve of, so I mostly stay out of here. I'd advise you to do the same."

I found the whole encounter with the West Wing depressing.

"Why show me this wing if I won't be working here?"

"I'm only showing you this wing's exit doors because it is part of the new employee orientation tour, and I'm required to show it to you. The staff to patient ratio here on this wing is very high. If there is ever a fire or tornado, it is part of the required emergency response plan. After evacuating and securing the patients of the East Wing, staff who work there must come over and assist the West Wing staff in getting these residents to safety as they are all confined to their beds or are incapacitated in some manner and require constant, around the clock care."

As we traversed the long hall, I noticed Dianna hadn't opened any of the closed patient room's doors. Given the moans, the strong smell of ammonia and pine cleaner that pervaded the hall, I was glad the doors stayed closed.

At the end of the hall, I noticed a spot on the wall that had an odd door.

"What's this?" I asked, confused as to why anyone would mount a door sideways at waist height.

Dianna stopped walking. A shudder went through her body, and I swear I saw her baby roll under the garish green scrub uniform stretched taut over her protruding stomach.

"That's a dumbwaiter, a leftover from when this place was a T.B. sanitarium. They used to transport the bodies down to the morgue in the basement using that shaft."

"They dropped bodies down a chute?" I stepped closer to examine, but not touch the strange door.

"Not exactly. That set up is from a time when they didn't have electric elevators and couldn't be seen carting dead people through the halls. Bad for patient morale and all. I'm told there is a pulley system in the basement for raising and lowering that platform once they put the bodies in there."

I continued to peer quizzically at the oddly placed sideways door, imagining the bottom hinged door being pulled down. *Did someone have to go inside with the body to ride with it down to the morgue?*

A tinny sound appeared to be coming from inside the body transport chute. When I turned to ask Dianna about the noise, she was already leaving the area. I had a hard time keeping up with her as she ran back to the nurses' desk on our wing in record time.

Three women in the nurse's aide blue scrub uniforms were milling around the desk. Two were sitting on rolling desk chairs, writing notes in notebooks they had pulled off a bookshelf from behind the desk. One of the younger scrub garbed women, one with pinked tipped black hair and a nose ring, was chatting into an iPhone. She turned away from us when she saw us approach the desk.

"Nikki," said Dianna in a tone that sounded more of a reprimand than an address.

The young woman with pink hair tips and nose ring connecting both nostrils hastily said into her phone, "gotta go." She turned back to us and said, "yeah?" in a tone that said she knew Dianna had addressed her as a reprimand.

Dianna smiled at me and explained, "I have to get ready to pass meds. Nikki's been employed here a couple of years and knows the ropes." Then her smile evaporated, and she turned to Nikki.

"Looks like you're free. I need for you to show Regina where the girls who room here sleep and help her get acquainted with the routine around here."

Nikki shrugged and said, "Sure. But this better not count as my break."

Nikki didn't acknowledge or even look at me as she took off down a side hallway I'd previously not noticed. I followed, unsure of my welcome. At the end of that hall, we came to another "Keep Out" sign, but that didn't stop Nikki. She took out a ring of keys and held a little fob up to a plate in the wall. Reminiscent of Gordon's apartment, I could hear the door unlatch. Nikki yanked on the handle and stepped over the threshold. I followed.

If I thought the main areas of the center were barren and run down, stepping through that door was like stepping into a reverse Wizard of Oz scene as we stepped into black, white, and dingy.

Or, at least the walls were probably once white, or at best beige. The wood stain on the plank flooring had darkened to black.

We traversed the long hallway that Nikki told me was the South Wing, or the "un-renovated" part of the Center.

The parts I'd seen were already renovated?

The hall in this section was narrower, back from a time when fire codes didn't require everyone to have unobstructed access to get out of the building. A few old gurneys lined the sides of the hall. Nikki shoved aside an old wicker wheelchair with the bottom rotted out. When the chair hit the wall, and a wheel fell off, Nikki just kept on walking.

The rooms we passed appeared empty of everything but cobwebs and dirt; most of their doors had been removed from their hinges and lay up against the walls of the hallway. They were once patient rooms.

We stopped beside a row of gym lockers next to a room that still had a splintered wooden door attached to its rusty hinges. My tour guide swung open the creaky door to reveal a room with falling ceiling plaster and cracked walls.

"Oh my," I said when I saw four beds, three unmade and rumpled, one with a stack of sheets on top of a plastic coated mattress. Four tiny nightstands were jammed into the room next to the beds. There were rusted ceiling mounted railings circling each bed. I presumed the curtains shoved off next to the walls were still functional and used to separate each bed into a modicum of privacy.

Nikki pointed to the plastic mattressed bed with the stack of sheets on top. "That'd be your bed and area."

She turned back to study my distraught face. "Yeah, it's a shit hole, and you've got the worst bed in the room. I recommend you find a room to rent in town as soon as you can. This room here is for the girls from the East Wing who are working the 12-hour shifts during the day. The room next to this one is for the East Wing girls working the night shift, then if you go farther on down the hall you'll find two rooms for the girls who work the West Wing; those rooms are even crappier than this one. These four rooms are the only rooms being used in this section, so if you think it's creepy and crappy now, you should see this area at night.

"Sorry to tell you, but after a day or two of training, you'll be in the night worker's room next door and will have to try to sleep during the day. Try to get as much sleep as you can while you're on the day shift."

"Why?"

"Why try to sleep while you can?"

"No. Why will I be switched to the night shift?"

"Everybody gets assigned to the night shift after orientation and training."

"Why?"

She huffed as if I was a petulant child. "Because the night

shift is bad. No one wants to work it. Did you already sign the contract?" she asked me.

"No. I didn't sign a contract. I signed a letter of commitment."

"Same thing. It said you'd accept any assignment. If you don't, you'll be paying them a ton of money if you back out before your six-month 'commitment' is up." She used air quotes when she said commitment. "Oh, I probably shouldn't tell you about working nights, but you'll find out sooner or later. Probably better to know now."

She leaned in towards me and said conspiratorially, "there are strange goings on at night. Some say it's the ghosts of all the soldiers who died here." She put her cupped hand up to my ear and leaned in even closer, even though there was no one else in the room. "I know it's aliens."

"Illegal workers?" I asked.

"No. Not green cardholders. We got plenty of them here. They staff the entire West Wing with them. I'm talking about outer space aliens."

I pulled away from her, shocked that anyone believed in little green men. "Why would you think that?"

"Well, we're out here in a desolate area near an air guard base. A few of the patients say they hear and see strange things outside at night. I used to brush it off as dementia, until one night while working the night shift I went outside by myself to get a quick smoke in. I heard a whirring sound. The outside floodlights are all burned out so I couldn't see clearly, but about 20 yards out I saw strange colored lights swirling around just above the ground." A shudder shook her shoulders. "Scared me shitless."

I shuddered just to see her shudder. "Did you ever see that again?"

"No." She shook her head emphatically. "I gave up smoking until I could get assigned to the day shift."

After I'd stowed my belongings in a hall locker near the

live-in worker rooms, I spent the remainder of the day following Nikki around doing on-the-job training.

She showed me all the essentials like where the kitchen was for filling water pitchers, where to dump the trash and dirty linen, how to make sure everyone was in the dining room for lunch, and other aide type duties.

I looked at the residents all seated around circular dining tables. Some had adult bibs tied under chins, some were well enough to have napkins draped across their laps. All were eagerly awaiting lunch. There were no empty seats to be seen.

My stomach growled. "Where and when do the employees eat?"

"You expecting to eat here?" Nikki asked me.

"The ad said free room and board."

"Nothing free about the room or the boards," Nikki told me. "This place will nickel and dime you out of your paycheck if you let them. They don't technically charge you for the room, just everything you need to stay in it. They allow you one free meal a day in an employee lunchroom through that door." She pointed to a door off to the side of the kitchen. "Mostly just leftovers from the day before that aren't fit to eat. If you eat more than one meal or take seconds, they take money out of your paycheck to cover it."

She pulled a power bar out of her pants pocket and showed it to me on the sly. "I learned real quick to bring stuff to eat with me. If you want to go get something to eat, I'll cover for you out here. Just make sure you tell the cook it's your free meal, so you don't get charged for it."

The employee "lunch room" was a table with two chairs, and a back access door to the kitchen. I looked through the window on the swinging door and got up the courage to summon someone, so I could order my meal.

Ground fish, ground corn, and squash were brought out to me on a small paper plate with one napkin and one fork.

I looked down at the white, yellow, and orange mushy

piles. "This is my free meal?"

"Yup." Said the woman I took to be the cook. "It's what was left over from the puréed diets from yesterday. You want something different?"

Remembering what Nikki had said about being charged for extra food, I responded. "No. This will do. But could I have a spoon and a glass of water?"

My stomach wasn't feeling too well after my strange lunch, so when Nikki got out the blood pressure cuff and said we needed to get vital signs taken on the residents who were receiving narcotic medications, I was glad we weren't doing anything more strenuous.

She did the first set of vital signs on Mrs. Jones, who behaved like a rag doll, passively letting Nikki lift her arm, pump the cuff up, take the reading, and then get her pulse; all without saying anything, directing her gaze at the wall. Seemingly oblivious to the actions being taken on her behalf.

"Next is Zina. I'll let you take her vital signs."

"Me?" I squeaked. I'd read up on how to take vital signs, but I'd never done it before. The error of my disguise was becoming apparent.

"Of course you. You'll be doing this tomorrow, so you need to know how we record the numbers on the chart."

I took the cuff, and after figuring out which way was up, I wrapped it around Zina's small arm. Nikki handed me the stethoscope from around her neck. I placed the disk in the crook of Zina's arm, the earpieces in my ears like I'd seen on the internet, and listened.

"You need to pump the cuff up first."

"Oh, right." Embarrassment flooded my face red at my forgetting to pump the cuff up. "I was just lost in thought there for a moment." I squeezed the bulb on the cuff like I'd seen Nikki do. The numbers on the dial of the cuff rose to 300.

Zina's eyes bulged out a bit, and she said, "Ouch, No one else squeezes so hard."

"Sorry," I mumbled trying to remember what I'd read about taking blood pressures. I turned the screw on the bulb, and all the air came rushing out of the cuff. I hadn't heard any of the blips at all.

"Is it good?" Miss Flowers asked me with a hint of anxiety in her voice.

Before I had time to think up an answer, Nikki said to me, "Wow, you're fast. Now you need to record the reading over here on the wall."

Embarrassed that I'd not gotten any reading at all, I stared at the long list of blood pressure readings for the entire month that had been written on a paper graph taped to the wall. All the readings had similar numbers and none varied by more than a few numbers. I closed my eyes and said a silent prayer that Miss Flowers's blood pressure had not changed, and then I opened my eyes and wrote down the same numbers as the previous day's. I vowed to get the cuff when no one was looking and practice on myself until I was sure my ineptitude wouldn't kill anyone.

I was exhausted at the end of the day shift and just wanted to have a hot cocoa, a bath, a warm bed to crawl into, and an excellent book to read, but that wasn't going to happen. Mrs. Mulgrew had summoned me to her office at the end of shift. Seems I had to fill out employment paperwork on my own time.

I had just started on the forms when the man named Mark from the West Wing came into the office and pulled Mrs. Mulgrew outside of her office. After a brief spell, she came back in and told me she was leaving to attend to a problem. I was to place the paperwork on top of her desk when I was done. Then she was gone.

I was sitting in the visitor's chair off to the side of the desk to write, but since I was tired, and Mrs. Mulgrew was gone, and her chair was padded leather, I sat down at her desk chair began again to fill out the forms she had provided me with.

One was a privacy act agreement warning me that I was not authorized to discuss any aspect of my employment with anyone, not even the other employees. I didn't want anyone to know I even worked here so that one was easy for me to sign.

Another form was an agreement to work five 12-hour shifts at straight pay before being granted two days off. I figured most people worked five days a week, so I signed that form, too.

Next, there was a form attesting to my receiving on-the-job training and holding the facility harmless in the event of an accident or other misfortune. I had some consternation over signing this form and decided since I was signing a fake name the form would probably be legally null and void, so I signed.

I labored over whom to put down as my "emergency contact" on the emergency information card. It was difficult to make up credible information without using anything or anyone connected to my real life. I wanted to write Frances Jonathan Bachman on the emergency contact line just to have the pleasure of writing Frank's name, but the pen ran out of ink after I wrote "Fran" on the line.

There weren't any other ink pens on the cleared desktop, so of course I had to look in the desk.

The central drawer had papers and bills stacked inside. On top of the stack was what looked like a billing paper with Chinese characters on it. I felt a wave of nostalgia for Keiko, my Japanese former maid. Unlike her, I couldn't read kanji, so I shoved that bill aside to continue my pen search. One of the drawers was locked, so I moved on to the other drawers. I finally found a black ink pen under a stack of pharmacy billing statements at the bottom of one of the side drawers.

I smoothed the emergency information form out on the desktop. I decided not to finish writing Frank's name on the contact line. Instead, I blackened out the Fran I had already written, and next to it, I wrote my emergency contact as

Timothy E. Warren, father. It felt good to write that even if I had to make up a fictitious phone number and address for him. Once all the blanks and lines on all the forms were filled with creative fiction, I placed the ink pen back in the drawer, stacked all the completed forms together in a neat pile on top of the desk, yawned and headed off to find my sleeping quarters.

By the time I got to my assigned room, my roommates had already pulled the curtains around their beds. I tried to unpack quietly and take Nikki's advice to try to get some sleep before my next shift began. I wondered who my roommates were and what else was behind those drawn curtains. I followed suit, pulled the curtains around my single old-style hospital bed, and lay down fully clothed, hoping that no one had died in the bed assigned to me.

Rather than sleep, my brain just wanted to think about Gordon, dead Lana, the Russian agent who had come after me, and Mr. Anderson, the mysterious CIA boss man I had to get to open up to me. He was close by, and he held the key to my getting my father's name cleared and the Russians off my tail. I had to get into his room. He had to help me. He just had to.

Before long, my thoughts began to drift to Frank and the feel of his lips on mine just before we left the hotel. His first kiss was so gentle that I had been disappointed. No woman wants the man she loves to kiss her like a sister. When I had found the edge of his polo shirt, I'd loosened it and ran my hands up inside. I'd tentatively stuck the tip of my tongue in his mouth and gotten a massive jolt through my system when he began kissing and fondling me back with unchecked eagerness.

After a few minutes, he had stopped, drew in a ragged breath, and pulled me so tightly to him that I had had no doubt that he did not consider me like a sister.

After he'd held me like that for a long moment, he had let out a breath, given my shoulders a gentle squeeze, placed a light kiss on the tip of my nose, and pulled away.

I had tried to return to his embrace, but he'd gently nudged me away from him and said, "I wish it weren't like this, but the fact remains that I've got to get you out of here. Just being here in a room that Gordon rented puts you in danger. If someone is tracking him, knows about him..."

When he stepped completely away, breaking contact, my entire front side had gone cold.

He'd grabbed up the leather jacket draped across the bed. "I'll drive you to your house and make sure you get inside okay. Then I have to get back to work. I'm already AWOL and have a lot of explaining to do. Staying away longer so I can make love to you is not going to look good on my record."

CHAPTER 11

I wished with all my heart that I could have been AWOL with Frank. I wanted to be anywhere but where I was. The slight snore coming from the curtain-enclosed bed next to mine told me the occupant nearest me was fast asleep and harmless, but I couldn't get over the fact that I was in a room with three other sleeping human beings, total strangers.

Try as I might, I couldn't get my brain to shut down. It kept returning to the events of the past week and everything Nikki had told me. I had gone from being securely ensconced in my mansion to sleeping in a room where people most probably had died, surrounded by strangers. As bad as that was, the real stay-up-all-night vulnerability issue that kept me awake was that the room I was in had no lock on the door.

I turned over, pulled the scratchy woolen army blanket around my shoulders, and tucked it around my legs as though that could protect me from ghosts and goblins.

I slept fitfully and morning came way too early. The shower water was cold. I'd forgotten to pack my toothpaste. The stack of linens they'd given me lacked a washcloth. I shivered all the way through my morning routine of fixing my hair and brushing my teeth with tap water. I put on the baby blue scrub uniform I'd been issued. The pants were way too long, so I rolled them up. The sleeves were too short.

Will anyone notice that I've put my sweatshirt underneath my uniform to ward off the chill?

I needn't have worried. As I entered the conference room for the morning report, no one even glanced up at me.

Since I was always nervous interacting with people, I held back from taking a seat around the oval conference table where six women were already seated. Two of the women were very young, almost appearing to be high schoolers, except their creamy brown skin was blemish free, and their downcast eyes were not focusing on smartphones.

I recognized Nikki among the other three other women. I chose a chair off to the side of the room, out of the way, but when the nurse in charge began giving the morning report, I had to scoot my chair closer to the table to hear her.

A funny little nurse in an old-fashioned white nurse's uniform, white sweater, white stockings, and shoes moved her chair aside to open up a spot as she waved me up next to her at the table. She took a cigarette out of a little pouch and pressed it to her thin, wrinkled red lips, sucking hard.

"No smoking in the buildings, Bishop. You'll need to wait until the break and go outside," said the nurse giving the report.

"It's an e-cigaretter," said the red lips I presumed belonged to 'Bishop.' "No smoke. No smoke, so it's legal indoors. That gazebo they put up for the smokers is too far from the building for my comfort."

She held up her wand to make sure we all saw her e-cigaretter. "I got this little baby so I wouldn't ever have to go outside this building except to go home." She gave a little shiver, pulled her white sweater closed and buttoned it up to the top button.

I listened intently to what was being said about the

residents. As Bishop hurried through the list of names most of what she said was "Unchanged, unchanged, unchanged." Until she got to Rorry, the young man who was recovering from an accidental fall off a building.

"Rorry has been complaining a lot of pain in his arm and legs. Since his broken jaw isn't due to be unwired soon, Doctor Johnson has upped his prescription for liquid morphine. He's to get it every four hours. Once the wires are off, and he can take pills, he'll be switched to Norco for pain."

"Lucky him," said one of the older women with three chin whiskers sticking out and silver streaks in her black hair.

How can he be lucky with broken limbs?

After the morning report ended, the day shift filed out of the room so the night shift could finish their shift and leave. I followed close behind Nikki.

"So. What do we do now?" I asked her.

"*We* aren't doing anything. You're on your own. Didn't Bishop give you your assignments?"

"Yes, she told me I was to be the aide for Mrs. Jones, Mr. George, Rorry, Miss Flowers, and Mazie McGuire but I thought we were supposed to do them together. I was promised I'd get on-the-job training."

"Honey, you done got that yesterday."

"But...but..."

She stopped walking and turned to face me. "It's all pretty simple. Just consider them all babies who eat, poop and pee. You see they are cleaned up, dressed, fed, and fed again, then undress them and get them ready for bed. Next day, you do it all over again. I suggest you go get Jones up first before she soils her bed. You'll have a big mess to clean up if you don't get there in time."

I was too late. Mrs. Jones was lying in soaked sheets. I got my arms under her armpits to get her up on her commode chair. I took the soiled gown off and saw she was pitifully thin. I cleaned her, dressed her, combed her hair and put her in her wheelchair. Looking at the bed with its huge wet circle in the center. I gave a sigh as I stripped off the sheets.

"I'm sorry I didn't get in here sooner, Mrs. Jones. This is my first day on the job, and I'm not accustomed to the work routines around here."

I thought I could hear a metal banging sound but since Mrs. Jones didn't react, I ignored it as well.

Nikki stuck her head in the door. "Rorry is clanging the sides of his bed. Since his jaw is wired shut he can't yell so that clanging is what he does when he wants his nurse. Better get down there. Besides, it don't do no good for you to comb her hair, fix her up or talk to her. She won't talk back. Just sits there with her stony face peeing the bed like a baby."

Mrs. Jones, her face with its long slender nose resembling a hawk's, looked towards the door where Nikki was standing. Nikki didn't notice how Mrs. Jones eyes zeroed in on her, piercing her with a gaze of pure hatred. Once Nikki sauntered away, Mrs. Jones's eyes lost their sharpness and dulled. She moved her hand up to pin a stray hair up away from her face.

The clanging was getting louder.

"Don't pay any attention to her," I told Mrs. Jones in a rush as I pushed her wheelchair up the tiny table in her room so she could eat her breakfast. "You can't help it if I got in here late. You're not a baby, just someone who needs a little help. I promise to get in here sooner next time."

Mrs. Jones said nothing as she pulled the paper napkin off her table and spread it across her lap.

As I was rushing to get to Rorry's room, where I could hear the pounding noise originating from, Mr. Jake motioned for me to come over to his doorway. He held the edges of his open pants in his hands. "Hey there, girlie. I need help fastening my pants."

I reached over to grab the edges to bring them together and was taken aback when he took one of my hands and shoved it into the opening of his pants. Without thinking, I pulled my hand from his grasp and slapped his face.

"Say," he shouted. "You aren't supposed to hit the patients."

The clanging grew more insistent. I had to go.

Mortified at the red mark beginning on Mr. Jake's face, I looked around to see if someone had seen me. I shushed him. "Mr. Jake, you are not supposed to accost the staff either. I'm sorry. You took me by surprise. It was an instinctive reaction. Please don't tell anyone."

"I won't if you help me tuck my shirt in." He had a broad grin on his face.

"It can stay untucked, that's the new style," I told him, leaving him to rush down the hall towards all the clattering.

Rorry was all trussed up in casts and madder than Mandy when she loses at cards.

"What took you so long? I can't reach my urinal." He said through his clenched, wired teeth.

The offending container was dangling by the handle on the railing of the bed, just out of his grasping finger's reach.

Not wanting to clean another soiled bed I nudged the can along the rail until it was close enough for him to grasp. When he flung away the bed covers to gain access to use the urinal, I dashed from the room—glad he hadn't broken both arms.

I leaned against the wall just beyond his doorway and tried to control my out-of-control breathing.

Why did I ever think I could do a nurse's aide job?

I would have to tender my resignation after breakfast. It wasn't fair to the residents of the center to have me for their aide.

By the time I got to Zina Flowers, she was already up in her chair at the table in her room, a worried frown on her face, her trembling hand fidgeting with a napkin that rested on the table in front of her. Tears were imminent.

"What's wrong?" I asked her.

"The grim reaper tried to come for me last night." There

was a little twitch at the corner of her left eye that told me this was not a joke; she was genuinely frightened.

"Why would you think that?" I asked her, knowing how my mind always played tricks on me in the dark of the night.

"I got up to go to the bathroom, and I heard a noise in my room. I opened the door a crack and saw a dark robed figure carrying two scythes. He was over by my bed." She pointed to her nightstand. "Right there. Only reason he didn't get me was I was in the bathroom when he got here, so he didn't see me. I hid in the bathroom until he left so he wouldn't get me."

Her thin shoulders began to shake. "I'm afraid to go to sleep most nights. They keep trying to give me those pills to knock me out, but I've been hiding them in my nightstand and not taking them. I know he'll find me if I go to sleep."

"Who will find you?"

"The grim reaper." She grabbed my arm and had a surprisingly strong grasp for such a little woman. "I have to stay awake now that I know he's after me. Please don't tell the nurse I've not been taking my anti-anxiety meds."

I felt sorry for her bad dream scaring her but didn't think I couldn't oblige her request. "I can't promise that, Miss Flowers. It's my job to look after you, and I'm not certain it's a good idea for you to not take your meds."

She lowered her voice and asked me, "Would you want to be doped up on Valium?"

"Well…" I hesitated to answer her. Valium was a strong narcotic, like what I had been given when I was overcome with grief at my aunt's death. I hadn't liked the feeling of flowing down a river of nothingness when my world was upside down, so I vowed to never take that medicine again.

She told me, "that Valium is what they give me for my 'nerves.' Only, as upset as I've become, that stuff hasn't been working too well lately. I've been asking them to give me warm milk before I go to bed. It works just as well."

I turned when I heard the sound of the breakfast trolley's

wheels squeaking down the hall. I had to rush. I hadn't finished any of the morning routines I was supposed to do and I'd yet to assist my last patient, Mazie McGuire.

"I've got to go now. I won't tell the nurse about the medicine for now, but you need to tell your doctor you don't want to take valium."

I rushed from the room, and she got up and followed me out the door saying, "Doctor Bonos doesn't listen. He's always in a hurry to get out of this place. He just keeps upping the dosage when I tell him this place makes me too nervous to sleep."

Mazie, small, pleasant-faced and on the plump side of 70, was dressed in a floral print dress and looked like she should be in a Pillsbury bake-off rather than shoved in a corner room rounding the hall that leads to the West Wing.

I sat her breakfast tray down in front of her and pulled the cover off her plate of scrambled eggs and toast.

"Yuck," she complained. "The bread is always so stale it's a good thing it's soggy; otherwise you couldn't eat it. Break your teeth, it will."

I looked at the plate noncommittally, wondering if my noon meal would be limp eggs and soggy bread that hadn't been eaten that morning.

"Eat up, Mrs. McGuire." I inhaled deeply and said encouragingly, "It smells..." then I found myself at a loss for words.

What did it smell like? Certainly not eggs and toast.

I opened the little container of jelly so she could begin spreading it on her toast. "It smells like breakfast." Or at least the grape jelly did.

"You mark my words," she told me. "That Mrs. McGrew is so tight with the food she squeaks worse than a new pair of shoes." She pointed to her plate. "Look at the swill she feeds us! She must be shaving money off the top of this place to pad her pockets."

"Mrs. McGuire, don't you think that it's mean-spirited to say things like that with no proof?"

"Honey, you can call me Mazie, and I got proof. I can see the side loading dock from my window. Two days ago a food delivery truck from Mike's Warehouse pulled up and unloaded a bunch of what looked like food crates. Soon after that, a white dodge cargo van with Sam's Steak House stenciled on the side backs up to the dock, only they don't drop anything off. Instead, they load a few boxes in the back of their van and took off.

"I bet Grew padded the food order for the Center with steaks so she could turn around and sell them to local restaurants on the black market while we eat cheap hotdogs."

I didn't know what to say to that, except like Pavlov's dog I began to salivate at the mention of steaks and hotdogs.

She didn't seem to notice my drooling and continued on. "My sister and I went to Sam's Steak House yesterday. I didn't know how to tell if the steaks on the menu were the ones we were supposed to be getting for the center, but that don't mean they weren't and that don't mean there isn't something fishy going on around here. As soon as I get evidence of wrongdoing, I'm going directly to my nephew with it and get that horrible woman fired for selling off our steaks."

All that talk of steaks was ramping up my appetite. I hadn't dared request breakfast knowing it would poke holes in my already holey budget. I had hoped lunch would be sufficiently filling to get me through until I could eat the power bar I'd borrowed from Nikki for supper. When my two days off rolled around, I have to go back home and stock up on granola bars and protein drinks to bring back with me.

As I picked up the breakfast trays, I pocketed every little packet of jam that hadn't been opened and even drank all the unused coffee creamers.

I was surprised at how quickly the day and evening passed and how quickly I fell into a routine the next day. My co-workers in the East Wing were mostly local people, but there were a couple of workers from Central America who spoke only a minimal amount of broken English. They mainly just exchanged simple pleasantries when they met someone in the hall.

I thought maybe I should stop and converse with some of the other workers—if only to be polite—but I was so busy trying to remember my duties, everything I was supposed to do, and I had yet to figure out a plan to get into Mr. Anderson's room to question him. I didn't have time for small talk. Of course, I wasn't much for talking to strangers anyway.

As the day dragged on I was beginning to think getting access to the CIA boss's room was hopeless, until I happened to eavesdrop on a conversation between two aides in the main staff break room.

"Have you seen that nurse for the guy with the droopy mouth at the end of the hall lately?" one of the women asked the other.

"No. Why?"

"Take a look at her next time she leaves for lunch. She looks horrid."

"Huh? She sick or something? Maybe we've been told to not go in there for a reason. You don't think that guy is contagious do you?"

"No. I don't think it's that. His nurse is super jumpy and has a wild look in her eyes. That room is close to the North part of the building. I overheard her tell Grew she's given her two-week's notice, but might not even stay that long. She thinks there are ghosts that haunt this place and it's scaring her."

"What did Grew say?"

"She told her she should stay away from the North hallway; it's been condemned for a reason."

"Wow! That's practically an admission the place is haunted."

"Yeah. You should have seen the look on his nurse's face when Grew said that. I think that's why she's now hidden in his room most of the time and why she's threatening to just walk out. I saw her once high-tail it out of the building for lunch, and she looked like an axe murderer was after her. Other than occasional lunches, she keeps strictly to his room with the door closed."

"With all the weird noises at that end of the hall, I don't blame her for hiding out in his room. Plus, he's got his own television. He can't talk so he can't complain about what shows she watches. Since the P.T. guy left, she doesn't even have to take him to therapy. Just sit and watch TV, and wait for the night nurse to show up. I wonder if Grew would let me work a job like that?"

"Forget it. His nurses are all hired by the company he works for. If Grew'd hired his nurses, they'd all be Guatemalan or Honduran. That's all she seems to hire these days. Well, mostly."

Both women looked in my direction, and I buried my nose in the magazine I'd been fake reading and pretended not to notice their sudden attention.

"Well, still," said the one girl. "It's a ducky job for someone."

"Yeah, would be if that room wasn't at the end of the hall where all the ghosts like to hang out."

Ghosts. Weird noises. Frightened nurses. Mazie might know something about that since she was at that end of the hall. She also might remember the times the nurse left for lunch.

Before I could go order my free employee lunch, I first had to go see Mazie. She had asked for a second helping of tuna casserole to be brought to her room, so I brought it to her when all the other residents were in the dining hall for crafting time.

"Sit down," Mazie said to me, motioning to the chair in front of her small table. She closed her door, shutting off the noises from the hallway.

I stood, uncertain of what to do. Dianna had said Mazie was to be pampered and get special treatment but I was also to freshen the resident rooms during craft time.

"No," I told her. "I have lots to do, and you'll need to sit here at your table to eat your seconds."

My stomach growled at the odor of tuna and peas. Two foods I had heretofore abhorred, but now found them to be mouthwatering.

"Darlin', I didn't order seconds for me. I got the seconds for you."

I blinked, and saliva began to flood my mouth. I felt embarrassingly stupid. "I can't eat your food."

"Sure you can. I pay for it. I pay darn good money to have a private room and enough food to eat. Seems like I can share it if I want."

"But…" I began, hungrily glancing at the plate of food, but trying hard to look away and not succeeding.

"I know they charge the help to eat and then give them swill that isn't fit for a pig. You don't look like you could afford to miss many meals. Besides, I want to pump you for information so I figure it's even Stephen. I feed your belly, and you feed my curiosity."

I still had to make up beds and empty trash while the residents were at crafting time. I hadn't a moment to waste, so I sat down and began shoveling the limp noodles and tuna in my mouth. I mumbled around the peas, "What is it you want to know?"

"You've seen the outside of the building, right?"

"When the cabbie dropped me off I did."

"Did it look like the roof in the North Wing was falling down to you?"

"Let's see." I thought hard trying to remember which way was North. "I'm not sure I ever saw the North Wing. It doesn't face the driveway or front entrance."

"Next time you get a chance; will you do me a favor?"

"Sure," I responded, wiping my mouth with the back of my hand.

"Walk around to the North Wing and take a look at the roof."

I wasn't confident I'd know a good roof from a bad one, but she'd just fed me so I told her I'd check on the roof and get back to her.

I was so busy eating that I never remembered to ask her about the ghost noises or what time Mr. Andrew's nurse took lunch. Trouble was, I was so busy trying to figure out everything I was supposed to do and how to do it, that I also never remembered about the roof checking until I was in bed that evening, unable to fall asleep.

That evening, I saw the other three women I shared a room with as we all shuffled around each other in the large four-stalled restroom getting ready for bed. I would have introduced myself to them if anyone had seemed interested in knowing my name, but since they didn't, I didn't.

One of the women was older than the other two, about thirty, with rough, worn face and hands. She nodded when I came in and started brushing my teeth at one of the sinks, but she must have been more interested in getting some shut-eye, because she grabbed up her toiletries and left without saying a word.

The other two women were younger. One had a bluetooth device in her left ear the entire time she was doing her nighttime routine. When she spoke Spanish into the mirror, I wasn't sure if she was talking to one of us or someone on her phone. Since I don't speak Spanish and she wasn't looking at me, I didn't feel the need to respond. The third girl was a young, pretty blond. I found it odd that she spent most of her time at the mirror putting on makeup and primping her hair before going to bed. I got the impression she wasn't interested in talking either, so I didn't try.

Even though none of those women looked like axe murders, it was still difficult to relax enough to fall asleep in a room with three other women whose names I didn't know. That was why I was wide-awake at one in the morning when I heard the door to our sleeping room open. I held my breath. Everyone was already accounted for in our room. If someone was entering, they didn't belong there.

"Psst." A voice said in a low barely audible tone.

"That you, Ramon?" I heard someone in the room whisper.

"Yes," came the Latino accented reply. "Which bed are you in?"

"Over here," came the soft reply.

The sound of the curtain hooks being drawn along the rails made me wince, but I held still, not moving a muscle.

Footsteps crossed the room. The sound of a plastic mattress compressing let me know whoever it was had gotten onto the bed. There was rustling, and then the next sounds reaffirmed that Ramon had indeed been welcomed into my roommate's bed.

Unlike my two other snoring roommates, I was not going to get any sleep while Ramon and his host were awake, which from the sounds of it could very well have been all night.

Thinking maybe there was a lounge somewhere with a couch I could curl up on, or even a comfy rug, I slipped silently from the bed and grabbed my phone, car keys, sneakers and the scratchy blanket. Once out in the darkened hall I slid on my sneakers and began my search for a more secure place to sleep.

I pushed on the doors to the two rooms that housed the West Wing girls, but the doors were shut and locked tight. That didn't matter to me. If I'd wanted to sleep in bedrooms with people I didn't know, I would have stayed where I was.

I searched the remainder of the hallway. Most of the old patient rooms lacked doors, and the floorboards in all of them were dirty and some warped from dampness.

I ended up in an unused shower room I'd found down a short side hall. There was a full sitting bench in one of the shower stalls, and I was able to fold several old towels left there onto the bench to pad it. To my delight, the door to the shower stall locked. There was even an open area at the top of stall door, and a high set of windows on the other side of the stall that made the space seem less claustrophobic.

I folded up another old towel to put under my head, wishing I'd remembered to grab my pillow. That towel had an unusual odor. Not musty or old, just strange, like cough medicine. I pulled the plastic shower stall curtain down and laid that over the towels.

With the scent blocked, I managed to get to some sleep, until I was awoken by a strange whooshing sound. *Wap wap wap*. Colored lights were shining in through the upper window of the stall. Orange, green, red, blue. Then the pattern repeated.

I watched the lights strobing in fascination until they stopped. The *wap, wap* noise continued, however. I lay in my nest of towels, shivering with fright to think I might be witnessing a flying saucer landing on the grounds and not knowing what to do about it, hoping they hadn't come to abduct anyone.

Then I heard a high shrill scream like a cougar or bobcat, or a tiny child.

Breathless, I ran down the hallway trying to find a door or a window.

CHAPTER 12

I raced along the dark corridor shining my flashlight at the level where windows should have been. There were window sashes with the glass panes covered over by plywood, the nails hammered in tight. Probably the most secure job of construction in this section of the abandoned building.

I pressed on, running over broken plaster and dodging old gurneys, hoping to find one window that hadn't been covered and nailed shut.

Finally, at the very end of the hall, I found a windowpane that hadn't been sealed over with wood and nails, but unfortunately the glass had been painted black. I used my fingernails to scrape at the paint, but it took a long time to clear a space big enough to see out of.

By the time I could peer out, the noise and lights were gone. I could see nothing in the blackness. All was quiet.

Disappointed, I returned to my hideout, lay myself down on the hard bench, and told myself there were probably bobcats in the woods and not abducted people screaming for help.

I slumbered fitfully.

My phone alarm *bling, bling, bling*ed much earlier than I was accustomed to, so I shut it off and fell back asleep. Once I awoke and realized I had overslept, I tried to hurry around, but I was stiff and sore from the cold hardness of the bench.

By the time I hobbled back to the wash area to get ready for work, my prior roommates were already up and gone.

I took the world's fastest shower, anticipating the cold water this time. Then I pulled my uniform down from the hangers where I had hung it to drip dry over the heat register after washing it out in a sink with cold water and hand soap the night before. The Center had provided me with one uniform, and had a staff washing machine and dryer that I could use, but that required money to operate—which I didn't have, so I did the sink routine instead.

I was determined to find out the comings and goings of Mr. Anderson's private duty nurse so I would know the approximate timing of when she left him unattended for lunch. I wanted to get access, get the information and get out of the center before I had to go on the night shift—which Nikki assured me would be any day now. I dreaded trying to work all night, but maybe, since I hadn't been sleeping much at night anyway, working nights while the building was quiet and with less staff might not be too bad. I was afraid of the dark, though.

My oversleeping caused me to miss the entire morning staff conference and I had to start my morning work routine without hearing any of the details of the report.

The fresh flowers on the West Wing hall tables were puzzling. So too was the replacement of the tinsel tree in the lobby area with a real evergreen, although the ornaments were sparse and no improvement over the last tree. The pictures on the walls had also been straightened, their frames dusted, and the grime at the corners of the hallways had been ungunked. None of the staff were loitering at the nurses' station; they were all going to and fro like ants at a picnic.

Even Nikki didn't have her phone out.

The housekeeping staff was cleaning the handrails that

ran the length of the hallway when the breakfast tray trolley arrived from the kitchen.

I got Mazie's tray out to deliver first so I could ask what was going on. I had a feeling she always knew the latest gossip.

"The whole place is certainly abuzz this morning," I said setting down her breakfast tray and removing the cover from the plate of sausage gravy and biscuits.

"Yeah. There are more people buzzing around here then fruit flies around a rotten banana. It's because Grew wants everything in tip-top shape. She's got some hunk physical therapist she's trying to hire. He must really be a hottie if she's pulling out all the stops to impress him." She picked up her fork and got the food almost to her mouth before saying, "I heard she's using the money from the vacant activities coordinator position to cover the extra funds needed to get this fellow on board. If he's that great, I'm going to ask my doctor to order whirlpool treatments to help with my arthritis. Couldn't hurt to get some blood pumping through these old veins." She winked at me and began vigorously chewing her breakfast.

Before I could leave her room, she said, "Of course, I heard that Mr. Anderson's replacement nurse is also a man so maybe he's the new hottie Grew wants to impress, and my whirlpool experiment might not pan out. Anyway, it can't hurt to try."

I walked into Mrs. Jones' room and saw a long, white tail twitching from under the corner of her bedspread. Next out popped a round black and white face from the cover. Steady green eyes watched me as I sat the tray on her table.

"Mrs. Jones," I admonished removing the cat from her bed and setting it on the partially open windowsill and scooting it outside so I could shut out the chilled air. "I don't think they allow cats in the resident's rooms and if you keep this window open you'll catch pneumonia."

Before I left the room, I noticed that Mrs. Jones had the window back open. The cat had jumped up on the table and was eating sausage gravy from her plate. I pretended not to see as I headed out to get Rorry's tray to him.

I found Rorry sitting up in bed, both casted legs propped on pillows, the urinal within easy reach.

"What's all the commotion about?" he mumbled through the wires on his teeth.

"I think everyone is getting ready for some new physical therapist to join the center."

I plumped his pillows behind his back, slid the bedside tray across his lap, opened all the containers, spread out the napkin across his chest and handed him the fork.

"Great," he grumbled, and I couldn't tell if he meant the meal of biscuits and gravy or the fact there would be a new therapist to help with his rehabilitation.

I was at the nurses' station updating the charts on my residents when Mrs. Mulgrew escorted the new employee onto the wing. He was tall, lean, dark-haired, and handsome.

He was Frank.

I swallowed hard, shoved the resident's chart I was writing on into the chart stand and turned to find someplace else to be, quick.

Before I could make a smooth getaway, Mrs. Mulgrew spied me leaving the desk and called out, "Regina."

Slowly I turned to face the music.

"You seem to not be very busy right now," she said. "Why don't you show James Buchanan, our new physical therapist, around?"

My face burned bright pink, but Frank's expression gave nothing away when he said, "Yes. I'm anxious to see the place, Regina."

The way Frank said "Regina" had me gulping. The intensity of his gaze, the way his eyes penetrated right through my deception had me flustered.

"Well then," I licked my dry lips and tried to make the best of the situation. "I'll show you the resident rooms in the East Wing first."

I took my time lingering over every detail of each resident, hoping to wear out the anger I felt was simmering just beneath the surface of Frank's polite smile.

I finally ran out of places that were in plain view of the others around us. Rather than go inside the kitchenette—not wanting to be without witnesses to my potential murder—I just pointed to the kitchenette door.

"And here is the snack kitchen were we get the diabetics their bedtime snacks when the dining room is closed, and where we fill the water pitchers the residents keep in their rooms." I walked away from the closed door without going in, intending for him to follow me.

"Perhaps you could show me where the pitchers are stored in here?" Frank asked as he pushed open the door to usher me inside.

Once we got inside the stainless steel appliance cave, he shut the door and let the hot smolder in his eyes take over.

CHAPTER 13

I went immediately on the defense. "You're not a physical therapist, *James Buchanan*." I gave particularly nasty emphasis on the name. "So what, Mr. President, are you doing here?"

"What am *I* doing here? What are *you* doing here?" he asked me in a barely moderate level voice, and I was glad we were out of earshot of everyone at the desk.

"I asked first," I whispered harshly to him.

He whispered back—more of a hiss really, "you're supposed to be back safe at Apartment Fort Knox, remember? That's the only reason I agreed to leave you."

"Well, I'm here trying to investigate that man who knows the details about who stole the missile plans and framed my father. Something you said you couldn't do. So, what are you doing here?"

"I'm here because I...umm...Never mind that. You need to get back home before you get hurt. This kind of thing isn't something for amateurs. You've no business being here. You're not trained in undercover work. And that hair color shouts your presence to everyone within 50 miles of here. Could you be any more conspicuous?"

I resisted the urge to put my hand up to the bright

Christmas red strands on my head, self-conscious that I'd chosen the wrong color to dye my hair. "My training, my hair color, and where I work are none of your business. I want my father back, so I have every business being here. My hair and I are not going home. I am staying and doing what I can to clear his name." I reached up and smooth down the awful red mess I'd made of my hair. I must have left Mandy's dye on too long to get it this bright.

"You don't know what you're getting into. This is not just about your father. You have to go home."

"What if I don't want to? What are you going to do about it? Spank me?"

"Don't tempt me." He stepped towards me, and I was startled when he placed his hand on my butt and let it linger there. He began caressing, and the smolder in his eyes was replaced by a hot spark.

When the kitchen doorknob rattled, his lingering hand pulled me close to him and his lips locked on mine just as the door to the room opened.

"No fraternizing while on duty," said Mrs. Mulgrew, a scowl adorning her face. "You'll have to make out on your own time." She deepened her scowl in my direction. "You! Get back to work."

Frank smiled a sheepish, boyish grin at the center's director as he said, "I was just trying to see if I could steal a quick kiss from one of the ladies."

He winked at her, full of meaning and I about fell over when she smiled back.

I stood there, dumbfounded at her reaction as he told her, "A place this isolated must make for some lonely nights around here. No harm in finding a friend to keep me warm is there?"

"Well, don't let me catch you doing this again," she said to Frank. She totally ignored me as she smiled a goofy smile at him. "Your accommodations at the Hampton are more than suitable, and I can see to it that you are kept warm. Now, compose yourself and get back to work. We don't have orderlies so you'll have to sometimes get the more difficult patients to therapy yourself if the aides can't manage it. You need to go and escort Rorry Calhoun to his morning physical therapy session with you."

She rounded on me, and her eyes snapped. "Since you listed knitting as a hobby on your application, I need for you to run the craft session this afternoon. Seems our activities coordinator hasn't shown up or bothered to call in."

Mrs. Mulgrew straightened her form-fitting suit jacket by tugging on the hem with both hands. She turned to leave as Frank held the door open for her. He watched her walk the distance of the entire hallway back to her office. She didn't look back, but I knew she knew he was watching because she put a lot of hip swing into her walk.

Once she was gone from sight, Frank let the kitchen door close again and turned back to me and said, "That was a close call. I don't know who can be trusted around here, so I have to be careful and trust no one. That's why you have to go home. You don't know the danger you're getting yourself into."

My heart leaped in my chest as I realized he was probably right about the danger. We had gotten close to being caught at our subterfuge, but I was here for my father, and I wasn't going to back down.

"I know what I'm getting into," I told him, "just make sure you don't get yourself into something or someone you'll regret."

He looked at a spot on the wall high above my head. "We'll take this up later when we can talk privately—come to the physical therapy room when you get a break." He pulled out a pair of heavy rimmed black plastic glasses, put them on and stepped out into the open hallway. To my relief, he went straight in the direction of the therapy room and did not detour to Grew's office.

Realizing I was behind schedule, I rushed to deliver the rest of the breakfast trays, straighten up the rooms, and empty the trash before lunch. I was eager to get everything done so I could get Mazie's take on what she thought about Frank.

CHAPTER 14

I carried Elsie Drake's food tray into her room and set it down on the small table next to her window. She wasn't in her room. She wasn't in her brother's room. He wasn't in there either. I checked in all the resident rooms the length of the hall and asked staff in the hall if they had seen them. They just shrugged at my questions.

Rose, a tiny Latino woman, became animated when I asked her if she had seen Elsie and Andrew.

"All people gone," she told me.

I realized she was right. Except for Rorry, who could get nowhere without assistance, none of the residents had been in any of the rooms I had checked.

All of the staff but Rose was seemingly unperturbed that most of the residents were not in their rooms awaiting their breakfast.

How could so many residents have disappeared without anyone knowing where they were?

I raced towards the nurse's desk to ask Dianna what was going on, but I stopped when I passed the dining room where an argument was ensuing.

"I say we need more evidence before we do something,"

said a male voice I didn't recognize.

"Yeah, we need more proof," said a female voice.

"We've got a plan, so let's stick to it," said a voice I recognized as Mazie's.

I stepped into the dining room and found all the residents assigned to me, plus the others from the wing bunched around one of the round tables in the dining area. Some were sitting, some standing.

Mazie was at the center of the ruckus, calling for order. "Settle down. Lower your voices or someone will hear us."

When I entered the room, Elsie shouted to the top of her lungs, "Don't drink the water, Andrew!" Andrew may have been hard of hearing, but he was seated next to Elise, so I had no idea of why she'd shouted.

Every head bobbed up at the shrillness of her voice. Everyone in the room looked at me expectantly—everyone except Mrs. Jones. Her blue plastic knitting needles were clacking away at what she was knitting, Mrs. Jones oblivious to the commotion going on around her.

The residents who were standing around the table began to stream away from the cluster and out the door as I approached their gathering.

"What's that?" Andrew asked Elsie, leaning towards her, his hand cupped around his ear.

"The water! Don't drink it!" she shouted.

"Okay. Don't worry. I won't drink the water."

"It's poisoned you know!" she shouted at him again.

"What's poisoned?"

"The water! Don't drink it!"

Andrew rose and pulled his sister up with him. Both walked away from the table together, hand in hand. I gave up trying to follow Elsie's logic and told them both as they passed me, "Your breakfast trays are in your rooms."

"I'll bring my tray to your room so we can eat together," Andrew told Elsie as they left the dining hall.

I stopped to admire Mrs. Jones' knitting. "Why don't you stop your knitting and head back to your room, and eat your breakfast while it's still warm." Then I remembered she allowed that cat free reign in her room and warned her, "You should get back before it's all gone."

When she sat her knitting down in her lap, I couldn't help but notice the intricate series of knitting and purling stitches that made up the haphazard pattern on the long piece she was working on. It was simple, ordinary acrylic yarn available in any dollar store, but the way she had worked the stitches was mesmerizing.

"What a beautiful piece. Is it going to be a scarf?" I asked.

She shook her head, no verbal response given. She gave me a Mona Lisa smile, pulling her knitting from my fingers to return it to her lap as she rolled her wheelchair towards the door.

After she rolled out, Mazie was the only person left sitting at the table.

She smiled sweetly at me and stood up as though to leave.

"Not so fast," I said, stepping in front of her and putting out a hand to stop her. "What was going on in here?"

"Just a little project we're working on. Maybe I'll tell you about it sometime." She circled around me and left.

I wasn't upset with the residents assigned to me over their impromptu meeting. How could I be? They were all up and already dressed. I'd not made any progress on seeing Mr. Anderson, and the residents' early-morning meeting had given me additional free time for sleuthing.

I meandered down the hall towards the door where Mr. Anderson was residing with his special care nurse. Drawing in a deep breath, I screwed up what little courage I had in me, and gently tugged on the door. I opened it slowly, not knowing what awaited me but willing to face whatever it was.

Mr. Anderson was sitting up in an overstuffed chair beside his bed. His small table had been pulled up close to his chair, awaiting his breakfast tray.

He eyed me as I stepped into the room and pulled the door closed behind me. "Hello, I thought I'd stop by and see how you were doing this morning and if there was something I could get for you." I searched the room, looking for his nurse.

His rummy eyes looked at me, and he shook his head no.

Seeing we were alone in the room, and knowing I didn't have much time, I rushed to his chair and crouched down in front of him so I was level with his eyes. I cut to the quick and stated my business now that the pleasantries were out of the way.

"I know you don't know me, but I'm Timothy Warren's daughter. Do you remember him? He used to work for you."

He nodded his head, and his eyes blinked furiously.

"He's in a lot of trouble because he's been accused of stealing those missing stealth missile plans, something he didn't do. I'm hoping you can help me. He said you were going to see him with information about who you believed really did the theft, but before you two could meet, you had a stroke."

A head nod and blinking again.

"Do you know who the real double agent is?"

His eyes registered surprise, then he quickly looked around the room, blinking. His left hand came up, and he motioned me closer, mumbling something I couldn't hear.

I had to step very close and put my ear against his mouth to hear what he was saying, "MMM beee hhhhh ddd aggggg will."

"I'm sorry. I can't understand what you are saying."

He grabbed my hand in his weak grasp. His face searched mine. "MMMM beee hhhh ddd aggg will." He repeated.

It was useless for me to try to understand his distorted speech, and we'd get nowhere with him just blinking answers. I knew I didn't have much time before his nurse came back, so I pulled a small notepad and pencil from my pocket. "Can you write?"

He nodded. His right arm was folded awkwardly against him, so I placed the pencil in his left hand and put the pencil point on the pad. He began to move the pencil slowly across the page.

He and I both jumped when his room door opened and

his nurse charged in with a tray of scrambled eggs, coffee, and creamed cereal of some kind. I turned my back to her to obscure her vision of the stand, not wanting her to see me picking up the notepad and slipping it back into my pocket. I had to leave the pencil there on his table as she rushed closer to us.

"What are you doing in here?" his nurse bellowed at me. "Mr. Anderson is not to be disturbed. It's bad enough I'm stuck in this creepy, haunted place minding an invalid. I don't need people snooping around when my back is turned."

He swiped at the pencil, and it rolled off his table and onto the floor.

"I'm new here," I said, thinking as fast as I could. "I was just making sure all the patients had gotten up and were ready for breakfast." I gave a slight kick with my left foot in the direction of the pencil and hoped it had rolled under the bed unnoticed.

"This is a private room with a private nurse on duty. The regular staff are not allowed in here. Ever."

"Well, I'm so sorry to have bothered you, Mr. Anderson," I said, patting his unaffected hand. His hand turned and weakly grasp mine before he relaxed his grip. When his nurse came closer to set his breakfast tray on the now empty stand, I pulled reluctantly away from him and headed for the door.

I rushed down the hall to the linen closet. Not my favorite spot but it was private. I pulled out the paper and stared at it.

My hopes fell at the sight of only a few lightly printed, barely visible letters on the page. "She is Ru." A pencil line trailed off after those few words. That was all that was written on the paper. He hadn't had time to complete the note before we were interrupted.

I wanted to cry, but after a brief wallow in despair and disappointment, I began to analyze what I'd learned from those few letters on the paper and my spirits brightened.

Those six letters contained a wealth of information that could help my father. Mr. Anderson had used the pronoun "she." That meant he knew the double agent was a woman. The "Ru" also indicated the name started with a "Ru." That name could not be my father's. What I had obtained proved the spy was not my father.

I was thrilled to have gotten this far in my investigation, but if I was going to absolve my father of guilt in the eyes of the law, I needed Mr. Anderson to give me the full name of the spy. I had to find another way to gain access to him.

Word had spread among the residents about the new Christmas tree in the lobby with its cache of already wrapped presents, so after breakfast I had no difficulty getting everyone out of their rooms and into the lobby area to examine the presents, so I could make their beds and fill their pitchers with fresh water.

It was the center's policy to change the bed linens every Thursday as a matter of routine. Nikki laughed when I asked her for training on making a bed.

"Making beds is easy peasy. No one needs training for that—just do it like you do at home."

I could have done it that way—if I had ever made a bed at home. I'd only done bed making twice. Once to get the sheets on the bed I was supposed to be sleeping in here and again when Mrs. Jones's sheets were wet. Both times were total failures. When Mrs. Jones saw me struggling with the long, flat sheets, not knowing how to get them untwisted and the corners tucked in neatly, she rolled her wheelchair up to the bed helped me. She pretty much made her own bed.

Now I had six beds to make, and that was a lot of figuring out corners. I puzzled over how I was going to do that and still do more sleuthing to figure out when Mr. Anderson's nurse would be gone.

In the end, I decided not to take the time to get fresh linens from the closet like everyone else. The sheets all looked okay to me, so I straightened out the covers on each of the beds. It took only a short while to hand smooth all the bedding out to look like freshly made beds. If I was still at the center next Thursday, I could make up for my lack of getting clean sheets on the beds then and tackle that bed-making thing in earnest.

I was straightening the bedspread on the bed in Mr. George's room when I heard Nikki say, "Look out, Genie!"

I straightened and twirled around from the bed I had bent over just in time to catch Mr. Jake getting ready to pinch my behind.

"That's not nice, Mr. Jake," I said as I dodged around him to escape into the hall.

"Thanks," I told Nikki.

She shrugged it off. "He's mostly harmless. I just came down to tell you that you're wanted at craft time."

"Oh, I'd almost forgotten that Mrs. Mulgrew wanted me to lead the group in knitting."

"Well, you'd better get a move on. The natives get restless when they don't get to do their crafts and eat cookies."

"Cookies?" Being the fill-in activity coordinator for crafts seemed to have some perks after all.

"Don't get excited. The cookies are for the residents. We're charged for every morsel of food we eat."

"I was supposed to get free room and board for agreeing to work here for six months," I grumbled. "You'd think that would include cookies."

"Making us pay for everything is how Grew keeps us on as indentured servants. As bad as we have it, it's worse for the immigrants. They don't even have family here to sneak them in food, and most of them speak very little English."

It was hard for me to concentrate on teaching the knitting lesson when the residents were eating cookies in front of me, but with some effort I managed to get everyone to cast on 28 stitches onto their needles so they could start making a simple seed stitch coaster. Everyone except for Rorry.

"I can't use these things with one arm broken," Rorry said. "I prefer making the candy dots to doing this girly crap." He flung down his set of knitting needles and yarn. "Where's Pricilla, our real activity coordinator?"

"Yeah!" said someone whose name I forgot. "Prissy said she was going to teach us how to stamp little messages on the candy we made for her. Not this knitting stuff."

Two men I didn't know began using their knitting needles as swords to start a sword fight. They put on quite a show as the room erupted into mayhem. Soon, everyone was parrying and thrusting around the room.

"Stop that! Or you'll poke someone's eye out." I shouted above the din of needles clacking and people hooting.

"En garde!" the people around me shouted as I attempted to take their make-believe swords away.

"Help!" I screamed when a robust man and his friend got me cornered, knitting needles pointed at my chest. Knowing the damage a knitting needle could cause to one's chest, my vision turned to black and I dropped like a dead weight to the floor.

"We were just funning with her," I heard someone say as the fog in my head began to clear. Someone was stroking my face with a cool, wet cloth.

"I think she's starting to come around. You can all go back to your rooms now. Go on. I'm sure the last thing she wants to see is you two guys."

Even though the haze, I thought I recognized the Latino accent and the smooth male voice that went with it.

I heard a few more grumbles of how I wasn't able to take a little fun and then I opened my eyes to see a handsome brown-skinned man hovering over me. I gazed at his face, marveling at how handsome it was, until I caught sight of Frank darting into the dining hall towards us.

"What happened?"Frank asked, kneeling down on the other side of me. "I heard the patients attacked a worker."

"Nah, they just got carried away playing Zorro with their knitting needles." The man with the wet cloth continued to stroke my forehead.

Embarrassed to be lying on the floor with a man I didn't know leaning over one side of me with Frank looking anxious on the other side, I sat up, blinking to clear my vision.

Then I wished I'd not cleared it. I'd never seen such a sour look on Frank's face.

"It appears to me she's in need of a nurse." He took hold of my arm to help me up. "I'll help her to the nursing station."

"Chill," the smooth voice told Frank, taking my other arm. Both men forced me up onto my feet, each one tightening the grip they had on my arm and pulling me towards them just a little until I feared I was the make-a-wish wishbone from a Thanksgiving turkey.

"I got her," the man on my right told Frank pulling me a little closer to his chest. "I am a nurse. I was just assigned to do special assist for Mr. Anderson. I was on my way to his room when I heard the commotion in here. I came in just in time to see this beautiful lady turn white as a sheet and drop to the floor. Her pulse was steady, and her color returned quickly so I figured she just must have been overcome with the heat in the room. Or she's pregnant."

"I can't be pregnant," I said almost in unison with Frank's declaration of, "She's not pregnant."

I stood up, shaking both their grasps off me, ready to get back to work to dispel that notion.

"Okay. Okay. Sorry, man." The nurse threw up his hands in protest. "I only just got here. I didn't know she was your lady."

"I'm not his lady," I said at the same time Frank said, "She's not my lady."

"Suit yourselves." The nurse looked at me and ran a hand over my forehead and then smoothed back a wet red curl from my face. "You seem to be recovered so I should go change my clothes and report in to relieve Mr. Anderson's nurse. She wanted to leave as soon as possible this afternoon."

I perked up immediately. "You're one of the nurses for Mr. Anderson?"

"Yeah. I was just given the assignment yesterday. I drove most of the night to get here. This place is such a hidden spot way back here in the trees it took me a while to find the place."

I blushed at the mention of his finding the place last night, but seeing my chance to possibly get closer to Mr. Anderson, I pushed the memory from the room I shared with the other workers aside and did my best to bat my eyelashes at this new portal to Mr. Anderson.

"Well. I'm glad you found the place," I told him.

Before the new nurse could respond, Mrs. Mulgrew stomped into the dining hall, marched right up to me and with her hands on her hips glared a gaze capable of burning a hole in my newly cooled forehead.

I shifted uncomfortably.

"What's going on in here? Why are all the residents in the halls? Why did you release them from crafting early?" she asked me.

I saw my new Latino friend leave my side and noticed that Frank had also managed to slide out of the room.

Cowards.

I tried my best to explain to Mrs. Mulgrew that the residents got out of hand with the knitting needles and how seriously dangerous I thought they were—the needles that is, the residents were probably only partially dangerous.

"Well, clean up this mess, and you'd better find something for them to do tomorrow that will keep them under control." She turned on her high heels and stomped back out.

I brightened. If I was going to be assigned to do another day of crafts, I was going to work the day shift.

I quickly gathered up all the knitting supplies and opened the craft cupboards at the end of the dining hall to put the stuff back where I'd found it. I rummaged around in the craft supplies hoping to find something less deadly for them to do the next day. There were colored pencils, paints, scissors, chalk, some kind of weird granular powder in a plastic bag and these funny little tins with circular indentations—like tiny muffin tins for fairies.

Were they for making the candy buttons Rorry had talked about? How difficult it would be to mix up a batch of candy to put in the little spots on the tins? Maybe that would be a better craft for tomorrow than knitting.

Then I remembered my cookie baking fiasco and quickly gave up on the candy button idea. When I saw a bundle of crochet hooks and cotton yarns at the bottom of the cupboard," I knew I'd found a safe, easy project for the next crafting session. That being settled I returned my focus to getting into Mr. Anderson's room again.

****

Frank was scared of what he'd find when one of the residents came running to the therapy room asking him to come help because "the nice redhead lady was being attacked". Then, once he saw Genie was okay and had only fainted, his adrenaline slowed. Then he saw Ramon Gonzales close at her side, and his adrenaline sped back up. Frank wanted to wring that Romeo's neck when he leaned over Genie with his mouth just inches from hers.

What did that guy think he was doing anyway? He was on special assignment and should know better than to mess around with the hired help.

Frank wanted to pull Ramon aside and tell him that he knew who he was and whom he worked for, but then Ramon would probably guess whom Frank worked for and that might lead to Ramon knowing what was going on and the FBI investigation being compromised. Frank had been told he couldn't trust anyone at the facility with the real reason he was there, so he kept the knowledge to himself.

Frank just hoped he could keep from punching the guy if he found him hovering around Genie again.

****

"Hey, beautiful." It was the male Latino nurse from earlier, now dressed in the lime green uniform style scrubs all the nurses wore. He was standing at the end of the hall, looking in my direction.

I glanced around me to see whom he could be talking to. The only person in the hall was me. The male nurse began to walk in my direction when I pointed to my chest and asked, "Are you talking to me?"

"Yes you, Beautiful. You feeling better?"

I blushed at the remembrance of his hand stroking my face and hair while I lay beneath him. "Yes. I am. Thank you."

"Good. You seeing anybody?"

"Excuse me?"

"You and that guy said you weren't an item. If you aren't together. If you aren't seeing anybody, I was wondering if you wanted to go to paradise with me this evening after work." His accented English was easily understood, but I didn't know why he was asking me about paradise.

"I don't know you, and I don't know what you're talking about," I responded, confused.

"I'm Ramon, and I'm talking about taking you on a little trip without leaving the farm. You know...a trip to paradise," he said again, winking.

Or, maybe there was just something caught in his eye?

"I'm not certain I understand. A trip? I'm not good with travel directions."

"You won't need them. I'll take you there." His smile and second unmistakable wink I understood.

"Do you always proposition your co-workers the first day on the job?"

"Nope. Just the ones that try fainting to get my attention."

"I didn't faint to get your attention. This place doesn't seem to be able to adjust the heat appropriately." I began to fan my face with my hand as he walked up close to me.

"Yeah. This place is a dump. A horrible place to work." He got even closer.

"If you think the place is horrible. Why did you take this job?"

He advanced until he was directly in front of me, our toes touching. "Beats working the crop fields and dodging ICE. Not exactly my dream job, or at least it wasn't until I saw you." He leaned in close. I could feel his hot breath on my face. I flinched when he reached his arm out to place a hand on the wall to lean in over me, way too close for my comfort, although he seemed entirely at ease.

"Welcome aboard, Ramon." I ducked out from under his arm and gaze. "The only Paradise I know of is in Michigan, and while I might want to go there someday, I remember there's also a Hell, Michigan and I have a feeling going anywhere with you, might land me somewhere in between."

"Okay. Just trying to liven things up. What's your name, beautiful? No one told me earlier."

"Imoo...I'm called Genie by my friends. Regina by everyone else."

"Regina. I like that. It fits. You seem like royalty to me. Out of place here, but royalty nevertheless." He placed one arm behind his back, bent at the waist to bow deeply, and before I realized what was happening he took my hand and raised it to his lips to kiss it. "At your service, my liege."

I giggled at the ridiculous way he was acting, and a bright smile lit his face as he gazed up at me from his bent position. I made a display of motioning towards the shabby front lobby area. "Welcome to my palace, Ramon."

As I motioned, I caught sight of Frank standing at the end of the hall, watching our silliness. The frown on his face told me he didn't find our display amusing.

CHAPTER 15

"I only have 15 minutes for break," I reminded Frank when he gave up waiting for me to come get him and came to the nurse's station to collect me for our private talk.

"That's okay. What I have to say won't take long, and I have similar time constraints."

We went outside on a path that ran alongside the building towards a large pond.

I never did well with confrontation, so I prepared for it by playing through all the arguments I was going to give for staying at the rehab center. As much as I wanted to get back home and start investigating who had killed Lana, I had my father to think of first. I had to make Frank understand my reason for staying when he demanded again that I leave the center.

Except he didn't.

"I've been thinking about what you said about this involving your father. I know when I couldn't provide any help you were determined to help him, and that's why you came here, but I'm here now. There's more at stake than just clearing your father's name. There are things that I'm not at liberty to talk about, but trust me when I say it is too dangerous for you to be here. I don't want you hurt. I can't force you to leave—wouldn't force you even if I could, but I am asking you to think about going home where you'll be safe and leave the investigating to me. I promise I'll do what I can to get the information from Anderson."

We strolled along while I pondered what he had said. There was a wooden bench by the pond, and I went over and sat down on it. The sunshine was warm on my skin, and I could feel the cold breeze blowing off the partially frozen pond. A pair of ducks swam in the open areas of the water.

Frank remained where I'd left him, ten feet away from the bench.

"I'll think about what you've said," I told him. "But I don't want to talk about it now. I want to just be with you." I patted a spot next to me on the bench and watched as he walked woodenly towards me and sat down, looking uncomfortable, on the bench.

My heart sank at the pained look on his face. Not really pain, more like anguish. Deep anguish. I didn't want to be the cause of that look. I wanted him to know that I loved him, so I took the initiative and kissed him. His lips were trembling. When I put my arms around him I felt his whole body quake, so I let go, embarrassed that I'd assumed he wanted to be with me in that way when he so obviously didn't.

The ducks quacked, chased each other and splashed in the water. I laughed at their antics hoping to lighten the mood.

When I turned back to Frank, his gaze was off in the distance, and he was shaking so hard I knew that a reaction that violent was not caused by me.

Is he feeling the effects of the recent cold snap? We'd both grabbed our coats before coming outside and I was plenty comfortable. *Maybe he's coming down with something?*

"Just promise me you'll be careful if you decide to stay," he said, standing up his eyes steady on the water, fear ringing out in his voice.

"I will."

"I've got to go," he said.

"But...we still have five more minutes..."

And then, in a wink, he was gone, leaving me to wonder what was going on that would cause him to leave so abruptly.

I didn't have much time to think about Frank's strange behavior by the pond, because I was too busy making sure all the water pitchers were filled for my assigned residents. I had just filled the first pitcher when I felt my cell vibrate in my pocket. I pulled out the phone to see who the caller was. It was Mandy. I pushed the ignore button and slide the phone back into my pants pocket.

I was at the icemaker next to Nikki filling the next set of pitchers when my cell vibrated again. I pulled it out to text Mandy that she needed to stop calling me. And then I noticed it wasn't Mandy calling. It was Gordon.

Uh oh.

I looked around for a private place to carry on a conversation with a man who thought I was back in his apartment knitting. I ran down the hall and ducked into the supply closet, activating my cell on my run.

"Hello," I breathed into the phone once I got the door shut.

"Imogene? You seem out of breath."

"Oh, I was just doing a workout." I *was* running, so it was partially true.

"That's great. I know you don't have much room to stretch in so small a space. Maybe I should bring you a jump rope when I bring your supplies?"

"Bring my supplies?"

"Yes. I figure you should need some eggs, milk and bread and a few fresh veggies and meats by now. I'll be in the area in about five hours, so I'll stop and get the groceries and drop them off."

"Drop them off?" I cleared my throat. "You need to drop them off?"

I heard someone walking by the closet, and I grabbed the handle to hold the door shut.

"Yes. Of course. How else will the supplies get into the

apartment?"

The door handle started to turn in my hand, and I gripped tighter and held it closed by pulling the handle towards me with one hand. The door rattled as the person on the other side attempted to force the door open.

"What's that noise?" Gordon asked.

"Nothing. I'll see you in five hours. I have a cake in the oven, so I'll have to go now." I disconnected just as the door flew open and one of the attendants came in to get supplies.

Without apologizing for holding the door closed or even acknowledging the staff person, I ran down the hall thinking up a plan to get back to the apartment before Gordon.

I was sweaty by the time I got to Mrs. Mulgrew's office. I was so frantic I didn't bother knocking. I just barged in.

I stood stock still at the scene before me.

Grew's arm was draped across Frank's shoulder. They were face to face, but both stepped apart upon my entering the room, or rather, they tried to step apart. His nametag was tangled in the button on her suit coat.

I felt sick at seeing Frank so physically close to another woman, but I didn't have time to deal with that situation. I had to get a ride to my car and drive like a maniac to get to the apartment before Gordon.

"What are you doing barging in here? Why aren't you at work?" Grew's vitriolic tone caused me to startle, and I could feel a little tick start in the corner of my left eye.

"I need to leave right away."

Frank's face registered a bit of shock before that darned poker face returned. I cleared my throat and began to think up a believable lie, but couldn't, so I went for the truth. "It's my father."

"What about your father? Is he ill?" Mrs. Mulgrew asked me, stepping further away from Frank once the tag was free of her suit coat.

"It's a matter of life and death. I must leave right away."

I saw Frank relax as he leaned against the desk and folded his arms across his chest. I knew that he knew I was lying. Except, it wasn't exactly a lie. Once Gordon found out I wasn't in the apartment he might want to kill me or make me wish I was dead, and with Gordon—looks could kill.

Grew stepped over to where Frank had perched on the corner of her desk, and, looking at him while talking to me, said, "I suppose now that I have James hired and a new girl being trained for the West Wing we could do without you for a bit. Perhaps you'd like to do a night shift for me, James?"

"That's a possibility." His eyes gave nothing away as he gazed at her smiling face, returning the smile.

Grew turned to where I was standing.

I was fuming, my mouth open, my face flushed.

"What are you still standing here for? Go home to daddy, and close the door behind you," she told me.

I was still fuming when the cab pulled up to the front door of the lobby. I opened the center's main door and got through it quickly so Mrs. Jones's cat wouldn't duck into the building, like it had been doing lately to get in from the cold.

"No luggage this time?" the same cabbie I'd had before asked me.

"No. I'm hoping this won't talk long. I'll be coming back as soon as I'm able, hopefully later this evening." I settled into the back seat of the cab, clicked my seatbelt into place, and cinched it up tight. "There's an extra 20 in it for you if you can get me to the airport in record time."

He didn't even bother to give me an affirmation as his foot jammed the accelerator down and we took off like a rocket bounding over the uneven, pot-holed road.

Once we hit the smoother pavement, he looked at me. "You were in such a hurry when you ran up to the cab; I thought maybe one of the ghosts of the place was after you, too."

I straightened in my seat. "Ghosts? You also think the place is haunted?"

"Yeah. The last person I gave a ride to couldn't wait to leave the place. Said it made her skin crawl. Heard voices at night. When she went to check, no one there. My niece worked there for a short while. Said she heard strange moans and whispers going on at night, too. She figured the place was haunted because of all the soldiers who died there. Then when she started hearing slamming coming from somewhere in the north section, she left and said she wasn't never going to come back to that hole to work. She cleans houses in town now."

My mind began to race, wondering just what was going on at night at the center. "Did she ever mention seeing colored lights in the night sky?"

"Now that you mention it, she did. Said they were real pretty. All orange, green, red and blue. She ran to get one of the other staff to show them the lights, but by the time they got back to the window where she'd seen them, there wasn't anything there. She figured those lights was another ghost effect."

I felt better that at least someone else had seen the strange lights, although I doubted those lights had anything to do with ghosts.

I was in my car, racing down the I-94 corridor when a set of flashing, rotating lights came up behind me. These also had nothing to do with ghosts. I dutifully pulled over, and the state police cruiser pulled behind me. I rested my forehead on the steering wheel while I did a mental calculation in my head. A long delay meant I wouldn't be able to beat Gordon to the apartment.

Without raising my head from my steering column, I decided on throwing myself at the mercy of the officer and tell him or her the truth. "I'm sorry, officer. I was speeding. I needed to get home right away so I could intercept my father. I'll pay the ticket without a fight if you'll please just write it out quickly. I'm probably already too late."

"Ma'am?"

I looked up into the kind brown eyes of Officer Sawney, the officer I'd run into the last time I was on this highway. He looked taken aback when he saw the speeder was me.

"Mrs. Dalmat?" he asked to confirm my identity.

"That was my married name, except I wasn't really

married because he was already married." I began fishing around in my diaper bag purse to find my wallet and get out my driver's license. "I didn't know he was already married until he turned up dead and his wife tried to kill me. I'm trying to get that corrected—my name I mean. His wife probably is still in a correctional facility."

I handed him my license. "So you see the name says Imogene Warren Dalmat on my license for now until I can get the money to hire an attorney to get my name changed back. So if you don't mind, you can just call me Imogene Warren, or Genie."

"Ohkaaay," he tipped his cap back and scratched his head. I loved how his hair smelled of herbal shampoo whenever he did that. "Miss Warren. Do you know how fast you were going?"

"Not really," I lied. Well, not exactly a lie. When I realized a patrol car was following me, I took my foot off the gas, and when I looked at the speedometer, my car had slowed to 75.

"I clocked you at 82 miles an hour."

"Oh, my. I had no idea. I was so focused on getting to my father. It's an urgent matter of life and death. Like I said. I'll pay the ticket if you'll please just write fast. Of course, I'll have to mail the money in, unless you want me to pay it now."

"Are you implying you were going to hand me some cash to handle your citation?"

The thought of that stopped me cold. *Did I just offer to give him a bribe to take care of a ticket?* I vehemently shook my head no. Being arrested for bribery would mean another stay in a jail cell, and I didn't want to have to explain that to Gordon or Frank.

I felt a tear trickle down one side of my face. Frank was back with Grew making plans to work with her on the night shift. I gave a little "hic" trying to stifle a sob.

Officer Shawney pulled his cap back down and sighed. "Wait here. I have to run your license plates and driver's license. It will only take a minute."

I got out a tissue, blew my nose, and wiped my eyes and

cheeks in the few minutes he was gone.

He handed me back my license, his mouth set in a grim line. "You're clean. No warrants. No priors, no points. It's against policy and against my better judgment, but I'm going to let you off with just a warning this time."

Before I could thank him, he narrowed his gaze and stiffened his stance, shaking his index finger at me. "This is a one-time deal, so don't let me catch you speeding again. And slow down, or you won't make it to your father in one piece."

"Thank you," I mumbled, not waiting for him to get back to his cruiser before I took off, at the posted speed limit. Or at least, at the posted speed limit until I was sure Officer Sawney was chasing some other speeder.

I kept looking at the clock on the dashboard. By my calculations, Gordon was going to be at his apartment 10 minutes ahead of me. I could already see him giving me that look he used to give me as a child. The look that said it all and was enough to have me confessing to stealing cookies or reading in bed after lights off.

I screeched into the second garage where I usually kept my car and raced up the back stairs off the kitchen. I was out of breath by the time I'd gotten to the third floor. I had no time to waste, so, fortunately, the door unlocking routine went off without a hitch.

I ran to the well-stocked refrigerator and started grabbing items. I choked up at having to feed the garbage disposal the lunch meats, bread, pickles, cookie dough, and other foods, but it was necessary to make it look like they had been eaten so Gordon wouldn't know I hadn't been at the apartment.

I paused my feeding the disposal briefly to take a big bite of a salami roll. It was heaven.

I was downing the meat with the last of the milk that hadn't been dumped from the jug when I heard the door lock unlatch. I was in awe as I watched Gordon deftly disarmed his alarm system within seconds of stepping into the foyer.

Clutching two big sacks of groceries, he did a 360 in the

living area before stepping into the kitchen area and placing the bags on the counter. I spied a bread wrapper still on the counter, but a furtive glance around the kitchen told me that was the only food wrapper I'd neglected to discard.

"Imogene, are you all right? You seem flushed and sweaty."

"I'm fine." I choked out as I tried to swallow the last dribble of milk and set the glass down in the almost empty sink.

He looked around the kitchenette. Before he could pick up the bread wrapper to discard it, I snatched it up. Had he thrown it away for me, he would have seen all the other wrappers and discarded food in the trash, and the gig would be up.

He said to me, "Your neatness is impressive. It looks as though the place hasn't even been lived in."

"Well...I've been trying to not mess things up." That was true. I was good at messing things up, so I was trying hard not to. The fact that I hadn't been there helped with that. "Hmmm. Even though I know how safe this apartment is, I was worried about you staying here at the house. Has anyone tried to get in here since you've been here?" He asked me, his face expressionless.

"No. Not that I know of." Not a lie, exactly, since I didn't know what happened while I was gone.

"That's good. I was concerned that with Lana Macintyre's killer still at large you might be facing some difficulties. Before I leave, I'll just take a few minutes to check some things on the house surveillance tapes—just to be sure no one has been attempting to get in."

"House surveillance tapes?" I squeaked. *Did he have a system that would show that I had left and hadn't been there?*

He walked towards the bedroom, and I panicked at the prospect of being discovered for the liar I was.

"I don't think that will be necessary. I've been here the whole time and would know if someone was trying to get in."

"That may be, but something might have happened

while you were asleep and you'd be unaware of it. It will only take a minute for me to check on things and then I'll be on my way."

He continued into the bedroom and closed the door. I heard the slightest of hums coming from the room. I noticed the door had not completely latched so I gave it a tiny push with my pinky and it slid open a crack so I could see inside.

There, in front of the entertainment console was Gordon. The television screen was on, showing a picture of one of the basement windows. I was bound to faint if Gordon found proof that I'd lied to him about staying at the apartment, but the television screen kept flipping through the various windows and doors of the house, I figured it was probably just a secondary feed from the central security system. If he was just doing a quick check of the current security status, then I was safe.

As soon as the picture screen showed the back door, he pressed two buttons simultaneously on the control unit and the screen went blank as the set shut down.

I backed away from the bedroom door, so he wouldn't know I'd been spying on him. I also wasn't so sure he didn't have eyes in the back of his head.

When he came out of the bedroom a minute later, I was knitting on the third row of an intricate sweater pattern.

He casually said to me, "I saw Amanda and her brother Martin come into the house ahead of me. I presume you have invited your sister as a house guest to keep you company these days?"

It was phrased as a question, but I took it more as a statement. He must have waited for them to enter before he snuck into the house. I looked down at the floor, wondering just how much to reveal to him about adding Mandy's name to the deed to the house.

If he saw them coming in just now had he seen me rushing into the house just before him? What kind of lie did I need to tell to get myself out of hot water and keep Gordon from stopping my return to the Rehab Center?

Before I had time to think up a credible lie, he said, "That's good you are making amends with Mandy and Martin. Having more people around means those agents who were after you will have a harder time getting to you."

He made no mention of my leaving the house and returning. I was relieved I was off the hook.

Or was I?

"Does our house surveillance system have stored video of the exterior doors and windows?" I asked trying to sound interested, but innocent at the same time.

"Yes, it does, and if you are asking about the night of the murder, I've already thoroughly reviewed the tapes. They show only those already known to the police as entering and leaving the mansion, so the murderer had to be someone already in the house."

He went to the kitchen counter and began unloading the grocery sacks for me.

"Speaking of coming and going," he said.

Here it comes, I thought.

"I'll show you a quick way to get to the third floor without alerting anyone that you are doing so." He smoothed out the cuffs of his sleeves. "I don't expect that you'll need it since you're staying here full time, but it never hurts to be prepared for any eventuality, just in case you ever need to leave or come back unobserved."

After showing me the back stairwell--with a concealed little trap door that led to another partition up to the apartment--Gordon bid me goodbye with a promise to be back in a week with fresh food.

After he left, I lay on the bed for a brief moment, to stop my head from whirling and my heart from pounding.

If the surveillance tapes showed only those people already in the house, then which partygoer killed Lana? Is Garrett not as innocent as he claimed to be?

He could have tranquilized his drink himself to make it look like he didn't commit the murder. If he was the murderer, then he must have hidden the gun somewhere in the house.

He certainly didn't have it on him when he left for the hospital dressed in that ridiculous gown and booties the police had put on him so they could take his clothing as evidence.

If the gun was in the house when the police searched it, then why didn't they find the murder weapon? Or did they stop looking when I was arrested with Frank's pistol?

CHAPTER 16

Gordon's bed looked so inviting and it was ridiculous of me to sleep during the day, but I'd gone on so little sleep at the Center that Zina's trick of laying down on the top of the covers appealed to me. After a brief nap I felt better, and since I had no reason to linger, I got up and headed back to Michigan.

I couldn't understand why I was happy to be returning to that drab, dull building, but that was what I was—dizzily delighted to be returning to the residents of the East Wing. Or, maybe I was dizzy to be working undercover there with Frank. It gave me goosebumps just to think about working that close with him on a case, even if he didn't want me to.

The same cabbie as before picked me up at the airport, and we chatted like old friends as he drove me back to the center.

"I'm surprised you came back. I thought you'd gone home for the holidays. If you had any sense you'd be long gone from that place," the cabbie told me.

"The place isn't so bad once you get used to it," I told him, thinking of being close to Frank.

"I doubt I'd ever get used to it. I get scared of big old buildings at night."

"It's plenty scary at night," I said. "Even so, I feel sorry for the residents. I can leave if I want to. They don't have any choice but to stay there at night."

Before the cabbie dropped me off, he wrote his personal cell phone number on a business card that he handed to me.

"I own this cab and just work under contract for the company, so if you need a ride and the business is closed, call me up on my cell. I freelance a lot and don't mind going out during off-hours, even if it is in the middle of the night."

I looked at the name on the card. Touched by his thoughtfulness, I shook his hand. "Thank you, Mr. Hanson. I appreciate your offer, but hope I don't ever have to call you in the middle of the night."

He squinted into the setting sun. "Well, working in a place like this you just never know."

I got out of the cab and hesitated to walk up the steps to the wide front porch because I noticed Mrs. Jones's cat perched on the sill of one of the windows. Mrs. Jones had the window open and was leaning out, talking to the cat. Her hand stroked along its spine. When the hand got to the end of the tail, the cat would turn around, and the feline head would nudge the hand to start the next stroke.

"Did you like the treat I gave you yesterday?" Mrs. Jones asked the cat, who bumped and nudged her hand some more.

"I thought you might." Mrs. Jones smiled. "We hardly ever get decent meals around here, but I know cats like tuna, and you probably liked that casserole more than I did so I was happy to share my food with you."

The cat purred so loudly I could hear it from where I was standing at the side of the driveway. The cat almost fell off the sill when it rolled over so Mrs. Jones could rub its belly.

"It's getting colder outside at night. I'd like to bring you into my room to stay, but we'll have to figure out a way to keep you hidden because that woman who rules this place doesn't like cats."

I was reluctant to interrupt Mrs. Jones's enjoyment so I retraced my steps back to the drive to enter the front door from the opposite side of the porch—where Mrs. Jones wouldn't see or hear me approaching.

The path on the other side of the lawn was overgrown with bushes and brambles that seemed to claw at my ankles. The flowerbeds were boxed in by lumber that had seen better days as the rotting wood showed signs of insect infestation.

Movement at the edge of the woods caught by my peripheral vision caused me to scream. I could swear I saw a silver clad alien.

I attempted to run, only to trip on an overgrown vine covering the walk. I landed on my knees in the bushes next to one of the crumbling flower boxes. I tried to push myself away from the sodden ground. My hand sunk into the icy cold mud. As I struggled to get to my feet, both hands sink into the cold, wet ooze. I reached out to dryer areas beneath the shrubbery and felt something cold and fleshy beneath my fingers.

Shivering at the feel, I scooted and scrambled to get to away from the thing I'd touched.

When I was able to get to my feet, I saw a hand peeking out from the dense shrubbery, and could see a body hidden among the evergreens. I turned away and bit my hand to stifle a scream. Then I remembered that my muddy hand had been touching a dead corpse, so I let go of the scream and didn't try to stop it.

I followed the scream with, "Help! Help! Somebody help!" at the top of my lungs.

Nikki and Ramon came running from the smoker's gazebo at the side of the building.

Ramon went to where I was pointing. He removed the concealing loose brush from around the woman and bent over to examine the body.

There was no doubt this woman was beyond saving. Her head may have been in alignment with her body, her limbs, and clothing all perfectly straight like she was laid out for a funeral in a mud pyre, but she was stone cold. When Ramon felt her neck for a pulse the head lolled at an unnatural angle to the side.

"Poor Prissy," said Nikki, leaning over to look at the body

and then glancing away. "Who would want to do in our activity director?"

"This is the missing activity director?" I asked, averting my face from the cadaver as well.

"Yeah. That's Pricilla. She worked here about three months. Didn't seem very talented for an activity director. She didn't know how to do much, but Grew seemed happy with her work. She was likeable enough, everybody loved her."

"Maybe not everyone," said Ramon.

The side door of the facility nearest the kitchen popped open and out poured three of the kitchen staff. They began screaming, and then more doors opened, more staff came out of the building.

"What's all the screaming about?" everyone who stepped out in to the bitter cold asked until they saw the body.

"Ewwww. Is she dead?" someone asked.

Ramon looked up and nodded affirmatively.

Mrs. Mulgrew stepped out on the walkway and surveyed the commotion. "What's all this about? Why has everyone left their posts?"

"It's Pricilla. She's dead," said Nikki pointing to the body.

Mrs. Mulgrew came down off the path but didn't come any closer. She gave a cursory glance toward the body in the bushes. "Probably fell on her way into the building. If she's dead, she doesn't need six people attending to her. We have live people inside who could benefit from your attention. All of you get back to your workstations. The show's over. I'll call the police, and they'll take care of the body."

"Nice of her to be so concerned," mumbled Nikki to no one in particular as we trudged up the path and into the building.

Craft time conversation that afternoon centered on Pricilla. Everyone was speculating as to what could have happened to her.

"I'll bet she tripped and fell and broke her neck," one of the residents said.

A young Asian serving girl from the kitchen was placing napkins around each table.

"Could not be fall," said the serving girl going back around to set a cookie on each napkin. "I saw body dead. Bruising around neck." She made a motion to demonstrate where on the neck the bruising was. "Someone work hard to kill," she said, going back to the kitchen with the leftover cookies.

When the extra cookies left the room, I had a hard time following the conversation as everyone mulled over what the serving girl had said.

"Yeah," Mazie said. "I heard Prissy was laid out nice and neat in the dirt. Doesn't seem like it would be that way if she fell."

"Had to be a lover's quarrel," said Mr. George as he tried to untangle the blue cotton yarn he was crocheting with. "I saw her and the physical therapist together a while back. I think he must have gotten mad because she was always in Rorry's room. Must have lost his temper and killed her."

"Rorry can't even get out of bed. How could he have killed her?" Mazie asked, disgusted with the suggestion.

"Not Rorry!" Mr. George retorted. "The physical therapist. That's why he didn't show up for work—he's on the lam."

"Only problem with that theory," said Mazie, "is that the P.T. guy left a couple of weeks ago, long before Prissy went missing."

I took the blue yarn from Mr. George, stepped beyond his reach, and gently teased at the knot as I reflected on that information. Pricilla's clothing was dirty but straightened on her corpse. I had missed the bruising on her neck, but then I'd been busy screaming and too quick to look away to see much.

"First the physical therapist doesn't report for work, and no one can find him. Then Prissy is missing from work and shows up dead. I wonder who will be next to go?" Elsie shouted to her brother.

After her outburst, Mr. George refused the untangled yarn I tried to give back to him. He put down his crochet hook and left the room.

Everyone remaining behind in the room became sullen. Most didn't even eat their cookies, which I discarded in the trash. As much as I would have liked to eat them, it didn't seem right to profit from my predecessor's death.

When I cleaned up the crafting supplies, my stomach and I regretted throwing the cookies away. I searched the craft cupboards for the candy ingredients Pricilla must have used in the molds for the candy buttons, hoping it was edible in its unmolded form. I found several skeins of delectable looking yarn, but nothing edible.

Rorry had said he liked making the candy buttons, so maybe he had an idea of where the sugar was stored. Since I had to take him to his physical therapy appointment next, I'd ask him about the sugar then.

When I walked into Rorry's room, Mrs. Mulgrew was there, standing close to his bed. When I entered, she shoved her hands deep into her skirt pockets, and her expression looked like she'd swallowed something sour. She stepped quickly away from Rorry's bedside, yanked on the hem of her suit jacket, and smoothed down her already smooth skirt.

She said to him over her shoulder on her way out the door, "Let me know if you need anything else."

"I'm good," Rorry told her. "Pleasure doing business with you." Then he sniggered.

Rorry was adamant that he never left his room, except for physical therapy and craft time. If the ingredients for the candy pills weren't in the craft cupboards, he had no idea where they might be.

"Why don't you ask Grew? I'm pretty sure it was her idea for Prissy to do pills for a recreational activity."

Like I'm going to ask Grew anything.

Rorry swung himself over to the side of the bed and stood up on his two casts with the help of his crutches. He deftly maneuvered himself into his wheelchair without my assistance. He probably could have gotten himself to the therapy room without my assistance as well, but I longed to see Frank, so I wheeled Rorry to his appointment.

"How are you feeling today, Rorry?" Frank had on that ridiculously oversized pair of glasses and a suit of white scrubs.

The scrubs accented his tan, and my heart beat faster just looking at him. He pointedly looked at me before picking up Rorry's chart. It was clear to me he was not happy I was still at the center.

"I'm feeling great. Lots of energy," Rorry responded.

"That's good. I'm going to get you started on some hand exercises for strengthening your affected arm before we work some more on using the crutches properly."

I turned to leave, my job was done now that Rorry was there, and I'd seen Frank's face.

"Could you stay just a bit, aide?" Frank said in a serious, all business tone. "I'd like to talk to you about one of the patients."

Frank got Rorry started on hand grippers for his casted arm and then drew me off to the side of the room, out of earshot.

He said, "I don't like it that your still here, but since you are, any luck on getting access to Anderson?"

I pulled the slip of paper out of my pocket and showed it to him. "Some. He wrote this for me just before his nurse got into the room. I don't know what it means, but I think it's proof my father wasn't the thief. The thief was a woman whose name starts with the letters "Ru."

"That might not be a name," he pointed out. "It could be code or nationality or an organization. I'm told Mr. Anderson's nurse stays with him for all of his appointments, but I'll see if I can get him alone when he comes in for his therapy. As his therapist, I might be able to get information out of him without arousing anyone's suspicion. If I can get him to reveal what he knows, that will make it unnecessary for you to be here so you can go back to your hotel room and pack to go home."

"I don't have a hotel room."

He looked taken aback at that news. "If you don't have a hotel room then where are you sleeping?"

"In an unused portion of the center where they have the immigrants sleep."

He was about to say something when Rorry yelled, "Hey,

how much longer do I have to do this shit? My hand is getting sore."

"You can take a break," he told Rorry. "I'll be over in a minute to get you started on something else." Then Frank turned to me.

"You can't stay here at night where those girls are. It's too dangerous. You are going to get swept up in something you know nothing about. You can come back with me tonight and stay in my room where you'll be safe."

My heart fluttered in my chest. *Stay in his room? With him?* Talk about being swept up into something I would know nothing about.

"That's a kind offer, and I would like nothing more than to spend the night with you, but I can't. Besides, I'm not sleeping in the room with the other girls. I've found a better, more secure spot. It's not comfy, but I do feel safe enough to get some sleep."

"Hey. I don't got all day here," Rorry yelled.

"Yes you do," Frank muttered under his breath, before he turned away from me to go back to his patient.

CHAPTER 17

"What do you mean it's my day off?" I asked Dianna as I took the paycheck she handed me.

"Didn't you check the work schedule? You work five-12 hour days and get two days off. You could have gone home last night if not for your paycheck being delivered today."

"But...But..."

"Yes. Get your butt out of here. This place will get to you if you don't leave every chance you get."

I didn't want to leave. Not without talking to Frank first. I had seen Ramon wheel Mr. Anderson into the P.T. room. I had to find out if Frank had found a way to interrogate Mr. Anderson without Ramon being around.

I raced down to the P.T. room and burst through the door.

Mazie was sitting in the whirlpool vat watching Frank with a look I recognized as admiration. He was paying no attention to her attention. He sat at his desk, making notes on a chart. He had those thick black rimmed glasses on again. He squeezed the side of the frames every time he flipped a page. He took the glasses off when he saw me come through the door on the verge of tears.

"Genie! What's wrong?" He rushed to my side.

"They're sending me home!" I sobbed, trying to fall into his arms, but he didn't let me. He gripped my shoulders, and held me at bay, looking over at Mazie, who had suddenly started counting the ceiling tiles.

"Since you refused to leave of your own free will, I'm glad to hear they laid you off," Frank said.

"No. I'm not laid off. They're making me take two days off! Two days." I had no idea of why this was upsetting me so, but it was, and I couldn't hold back the tears.

"Well, that's hardly a criminal offense. According to Department of Labor standards, you should be getting more time off than just the two days, plus overtime pay, but I don't understand why having time off is causing you such grief."

"I wanted to make sure Mr. George got his dishcloth done for his daughter's Christmas present, and who's going to clean Mrs. Jones up if she has another accident? What if they find her cat and throw it out in the cold? What if Miss Flowers has another nightly visitor who scares her and there is no one to calm her?"

Frank put his arms around me and pulled me in for a tight embrace. "Genie, it will be alright. You can leave for two days, and these people will be alright."

"But," I whispered. "What about finding out who the spy is? How can I do that from home?"

"It can all wait. I'll do what I can from here. Go home. Get some decent sleep. Eat some decent food. Watch some television. Knit or whatever it is that you do with all that yarn you have. And, relax."

Decent food?

I suddenly remembered that Gordon had brought me his homemade sugar cookies with the groceries. I'd forgotten and left those at the house. Suddenly, I didn't feel like crying. I felt like driving home.

CHAPTER 18

When I got to the kitchen door of my house, I noticed it was not completely latched. I could hear noise coming from inside the house. Not being very brave, I cautiously opened the door wider and peeked inside before entering.

Scuffling and growling was coming from the laundry room, which was the warmest room in the house and the place where Mr. M liked to nap. I grabbed a frying pan from the stove and ran into the laundry room to confront whoever was trying to dognap my sister's dog.

Mr. M's teeth had a hold of a man's pant leg. He was tugging and growling. Mr. M that is. The tall man had Mandy's head in a chokehold. He was saying to her, "Give me plans or give me father."

Mandy was pulling at the man's arm, kicking and flailing around ineffectually.

I came up behind the man and bonked him on the back of the head with the frying pan. He let go of Mandy to grab his head. He spun around to confront me. He gave a gasp when our eyes met. Before I could hit him again, he shook his head and ran out the back door.

Mandy was choking and screaming at me to go after the

man.

As if.

Mr. M came up to me with his tail wagging.

"Who was that man?" Mandy shouted at me while I petted her dog.

"How should I know? You were the one who turned off the security system to let him in."

"I only opened the door because I thought he was Mr. Gildercrantz or Rosenttine or whatever his name was coming to get the name and number of the band Martin hired."

"Their names are Rosenthal and Guildenstein. And why would either of them want the band information?" I was having trouble following her explanation for how an assailant got in our house and his arm around her throat.

"Because he's a publicity agent. He said he was planning a book launch party and he loved that band...Never mind that, that man was trying to kill me!"

I pulled down the edge of her cowl necked top and took a close look at her neck. It looked okay except for one red scratch that must have come from the diamond pendant on her necklace.

"He kept telling me I'd better give him 'the plans' or tell him where my daddy is. I don't know about any plans, and I have no idea how he found out that traitor of yours is my daddy, too—he certainly couldn't have been referring to mama's husband. He's back in Georgia."

Seeing that Mandy was back to her old self in record time, I went to the kitchen to assure myself the assailant was gone. Then I locked the door and reset the alarms before I called the police.

I sat Mandy down in a kitchen chair to await their arrival. She was shaking and sobbing; most of it I was sure was for show. Her hair, dyed brown now, didn't even seem mussed, and her crisp, new clothing was only slightly wrinkled.

Sitting there, waiting for the police, I took a hard look at Mandy and began to see my sister as the assailant must have seen her. I realized then that with her hair cut like mine and with her recent weight loss, she looked very much like me.

"So did you get a good look at the assailant?" I asked her.

"No. Did you?"

"No. His back was to me most of the time, and when he turned, I wasn't thinking too clearly. I could see he was tall, dark-haired, and in a suit, but I don't remember much about his face, except he looked shocked. Did you notice any distinguishing features?"

"How should I know? I was terrified out of my mind. I don't have a photographic memory for faces. His cheap suit was off the rack, and his shoes were tacky and worn. That's all I remember."

Oh, Mandy *would* remember his suit and shoes weren't expensive. Why couldn't she once remember something useful?

"What color was the suit?" I asked since she was focused on that.

"Tacky brown. Who wears a brown suit these days? And he had on a black wool coat, with a black hat and gloves."

"Could you see the color of his eyes? His hair? The shape of his nose?"

"He was ugly. I remember that." Mandy stood up to get a mug from the cupboard. Mr. M. was at her feet, and he followed her over to the counter where she poured coffee.

"That man didn't hurt Mr. M did he?" I asked.

"No! He was too busy choking me. Mr. Mister was so brave. He grabbed the man's pant leg and gave it a good tug trying to get him to let go of me." She picked up Mr. M and nuzzled his face to hers. He licked her chin. "Mr. Mister was protecting me, and that man was shaking his leg, trying to shake him off, but my little hero held on tight. My little man was saving me from that crazy."

"You think he was crazy?"

"Well, he couldn't have been in his right mind to think Mr. Mister was a fish."

"A fish?" I asked, confused.

"Yes. He kept calling him a Chinook. That's a fish, isn't it?

Doesn't that prove the man's off his rocker?"

She sat down at the table again, picked up Mr. M and hugged him to her chest and then began weeping loudly again.

"I should never have moved into this place. You have such horrible friends."

"He's not one of my friends! Why would you think that man was one of my friends?" I asked as I began scrolling on my phone, looking to see if Chinook was more than just a name for a type of salmon.

I sat down heavily in a nearby chair, my legs suddenly wobbly.

Chinook was a Russian word for puppy.

Oh no! My Russian woes were not over.

A knock on the door had us both screaming.

"It's the police! Open up!"

Relieved, I rushed to open the door.

Once the police officers had finished getting the information from Mandy, I locked the doors, reset the alarms, and rushed up to my room to work on my desktop publishing program again. When I was done, I found a legal sized envelope and put it through the printer to address it to my sister. I didn't figure I had time to wait until it went through the postal mailing system, so I put a stamp on the letter and used an ink pen to put some squiggly cancelation lines over the stamp. I added the letter to the stack of mail that had already been brought in, sitting on the hall table.

"Anything come in the mail for me?" I asked Mandy, keeping my voice level with no inflection.

"I don't know. The mail's on the hall table. Go look for yourself."

I brought the stack in and began sorting it. Most of it was household bills, but there were one or two legitimate letters for Mandy, so I put the letter I'd drafted in between the two of them.

"There's a few here for you," I told her, flinging the three letters down in front of her.

She began to open the first one and flung it aside. It

looked to be a credit card bill. When she got to the second letter, the one I'd addressed to her, she opened it and began to sputter and fume.

"What's this? I thought my name had been added to the deed of this house. How could I be evicted by the city from my own home?"

"What?" I said innocently glancing over her shoulder to look at the letter.

"It says I have to be out by this evening. Something about the house being radioactive or something and not approved for habitation until the foundation is dug up and replaced.

"I knew it was a bad idea to move in with you! You probably knew about this all along and wanted me here to pay for the cleanup of your mess. How does a house even get to be radioactive? This is absurd!"

She grabbed up Mr. M and began rushing around, grabbing his bowls from the floor, his food from the pantry, and his water from the fridge. "We've got to get out of here! I need to call Martin and tell him to pick me up right away. It's a good thing I hadn't sublet my apartment yet."

Then, as if it occurred to her that I was just watching her and not making an effort to leave, she turned to me. "Do you want to come stay with Martin and me at my apartment? It's not safe for you to stay here. You might end up glowing in the dark or something worse."

She was right about it not being safe to stay there, especially when the Russian agents couldn't tell the difference between my sister and me, but I had Gordon's apartment to hide out in and an overall top-notch security system.

"I have someplace to go. Don't worry about me."

"Oh yeah. You have that FBI creep you can run to now that Garrett is through with you."

Once I had the house to myself, I was curious about why a publicity agent would need to know the name of the band Martin had hired for his acquittal party. So, not trusting Rosenthal or Guildenstein to have honest motives, I rifled through the papers on Martin's desk until I found the names of everyone who had been invited to the event.

The band's name of "Troika Troup" was on that list, but not the names of the musicians that played in the group that night. I sank down into Martin's desk chair and did some more searching through his things. I began to sweat when I found the billings for the food and entertainment and realized that not only was the band Russian, but the catering company was as well.

Were any of the band's musicians or the catering service staff Russian agents? How would I know if they were? How much of my resemblance to Lana and Mandy had factored into what happened to them?

I picked up Martin's desk phone and dialed someone who could do some checking on things for me. I only hoped the last check I wrote him hadn't bounced.

"Chilton Detective Agency."

"Milton? Is that you?"

"Yeah." A hint of confusion was in his voice when he asked, "Imogene?"

Usually, his secretary answered the phone, because he was always out of the office. "I expected your secretary to answer."

"I did, too, but she took off. I haven't found a replacement yet."

"Oh. I was wondering if you would have some time to track down some information for me."

"Sure. You wanting more intel on your not-so-dead father?"

"Ahh, no," I explained what I was interested in discovering. When agreed to help me, I thought it only polite to ask how he was doing.

"It's been rough since my secretary quit. I need to get another one or at least set up some type of an answering service so I can leave the office more."

Translation: He couldn't go to the bar when he wanted to.

I wouldn't lie to him and say I was sorry to hear he was forced to stay sober when I wasn't, so I thanked him for taking this latest assignment from me and hung up.

Next, I got out the guest list for the party and began searching through it to see if any names looked suspicious. I recognized a few of the names as being Mandy's real estate friends. I knew the name of Martin's attorneys, my aunt's publicist, and agent, and of course, Garrett, but the rest of the names were total strangers. I supposed, knowing how Mandy was, those names were probably socialites that even she didn't know.

Someone on that list had killed Lana. If I went under the assumption the killer had been aiming for me that left me with very few names to investigate, because if I didn't know a name on the list, chances were those names must not know me either.

Garrett had told the police his back was to the bedroom door, or rather to the ceiling, when he passed out, so he hadn't seen the killer, but I was hoping maybe he had gotten a look at them before he and Lana entered the room.

I gritted my teeth and picked up the phone. Garrett answered his cell on the second ring.

"What do you want?" he whispered into the phone, his voice harsh.

"I want to talk to you about the other night."

I heard a sharp intake of breath on the other end of the connection, and then he blew it all out before saying. "What about the other night?"

I gulped, "Is now a good time to talk?"

"Sure. I'm just on assignment guarding the vice president while he makes a speech in Detroit. He can wait."

I choked. I'd forgotten that the vice president was in Chicago to give a speech and had totally forgotten that part of Garrett's secret service job was more than just overseeing the security at the Federal Reserve; he also had to guard the president and his staff when they were in the Midwest.

"I'm sorry. I'll call back."

Before I could disconnect Garrett interjected, "I can talk. He's not arrived yet. We're all just standing around waiting for him to show up. So you've been thinking about the other night?"

His harshness was gone. His voice sounded hopeful, and I had a difficult time gauging if I should lead him on for the sake of information or play it straight.

In my usual fashion, I straddled the fence. "I have been thinking about it, and first off, I'd like to say I'm sorry for the events of the evening. It must have been horrible for you."

"Well, I was hurt."

Huh? "You were?" concern ringed my voice. I had been told the hospital checked Garrett over and then released him, undamaged.

"Yeah. I thought we meant something to each other."

Reality check for me. This was Garrett I was talking to. "I meant I'm sorry about Lana's death."

"Oh yeah. That, too."

Steering our conversation back to my interests, I asked, "Did you see or hear anything that might indicate who the killer was?"

"Nah. If you remember I was otherwise engaged when the tranquilizer hit. I fell over on the bed passed out cold."

"I'm glad you were out cold," I said thinking of the implications of him being awake when the killer came in. I hurriedly explained lest he got the wrong idea. "If you'd been awake and seen the killer, you'd have probably been killed as well. Eyewitness and all."

"Not likely. The forensics expert says he thinks the gun was a Remington Vest Pocket Pistol, a single shot unique handgun. Only takes one bullet at a time. That makes it very small, only a few inches long and easily hidden. Might even still be in your house somewhere since the police were looking for a bigger gun and might not have searched every crevice."

I almost fainted at the thought of whoever had brought the gun in only needed one bullet to do the job, and the job was me.

"I certainly hope not. I mean about the gun being in the house, not that the police might not have searched every crevice."

"Imogene, you're rambling. Normally I find that cute, but I'm short on time right now. Why don't you just get to the point of why you called? I'm waiting to hear how you've changed your mind about us, but I haven't got all day."

Oh, no. How was I to handle that?

"The reason for my call is…." I cleared my throat.

"Yes." The expectancy in his voice was daunting.

"The reason for my call is…" I cleared my throat again. "Say… I was wondering if when you were at the party, did you see anyone on your way up the stairs? There were some big names on the guest list."

"I did recalling seeing a few famous people," he began. "One of them approached us just before the bartender asked me to go get some vodka."

"Really?"

"Yes. Victor James came up to me and asked if I was the guy who caught the counterfeiters. He said they were thinking of making a movie of the attempted robbery of the Federal Reserve and wanted to get the rights to the story."

"Oh." I was disappointed. I'd read in the paper that Victor James, the movie mogul, had been cleared by the authorities because at the time of the murder he was being accosted by Mandy, his adoring fan. She vouched for Victor's whereabouts the entire time Garrett was upstairs.

"So, is it my fame that has caused you to rethink our relationship or are you missing me?" Garrett asked.

I was all prepared to tell him what I thought of 'our' relationship when I heard some noise in the background of his call, and he said, "I've got to go, honey. The limo just pulled up. I'll call you back later."

He clicked off.

I was ticked off. *Honey? How did he construe that I wanted to be his 'Honey' from my asking him questions about seeing anyone on his way to my bedroom to have sex with my look-a-like?*

I tried to find information on the band. They didn't have a website, but they did have a Facebook page. I saw where every member of the band linked their personal profiles to their business page, so it was easy to find the guy who was so concerned about his mandolin from links. I private messaged him asking if I could come and see his instrument.

Gee, I hope he didn't take that request the wrong way.

After I'd done all the investigating I could from my stay at Gordon's apartment, I pulled out some of the yarn Gordon had bought me and thought up some crochet patterns to work on. If I had to stay cooped up for two days, I might just as well find a way to be happy about it.

It was a rough two days, but thanks to Christmas being only days away I stayed busy. A shrug for Mandy, four dishcloths for Janey, ten slippers for my regularly assigned residents at the center, two pair of baby booties and teddy bears for Janey's son Johnny and Dianna's baby, a hat for Frank, and one very cute cat toy I dreamed up for Mrs. Jones's cat.

I kept the house alarms on and my phone off. That's why I never got even one of the many calls from Frank.

Mr. Hanson hit a traffic jam, so when he dropped me off at the Center for my scheduled workday I didn't have time to see Frank like I'd planned. Everyone at the Center was abuzz, and it wasn't because the next day was Christmas.

Elsie was missing. Her brother was inconsolable. He kept telling everyone he couldn't live without her.

"How long has Elsie been missing?" I asked Nikki.

"Beats me. She and Andrew were assigned to the new girl, Rose, who came over from the West Wing to fill in. She doesn't speak English. She kept trying to tell us Andrew and Elsie had gone off somewhere, but when she kept saying "Elsie and Andrew," we thought she was just complaining about being assigned to a crazy woman and her brother, so we ignored her. By the time we thought to have Ramon speak to her in Spanish, a whole day had passed with Andrew and Elsie lost.

"Andrew came back that evening looking dusty and dirty, saying he and Elsie had gone for a walk and gotten separated. He looked everywhere, but he couldn't find her. Elsie has a habit of wandering off, but she usually comes back with no problem. However, no one knows where she went this time. Andrew claims they got separated while 'exploring.' I'm beginning to wonder if he got tired of her shouting at him and…"

"He would never do that," I said, knowing how much he looked after Elsie. *Or would he?* I couldn't say I was the best at judging a man's character. After all, I'd married a conning bigamist.

"Have the police been called?" I began to have horrible flashbacks to hiding in a Laundromat to elude hired killers.

"Grew doesn't want to involve the police until after Elsie has been gone more than 48 hours. She says Elsie will turn up any minute, just as she has before. Except, Elsie has never been gone this long."

I felt my stomach churning and my breath catch in my throat. "Forty-eight hours! She could be dead by then."

"That's Grew for you. All heart."

Nikki walked away, but I stood there trying to get a grip on my emotions. This center was on 90 acres of wooded area. It was a mild December for the mid-west, but still winter-cold with the pond starting to freeze a thick layer of ice on top.

After making sure everyone assigned to me had been served breakfast, I went to find Frank. I managed to catch him in between therapy sessions.

"Genie!" He grabbed me and hugged me tightly. "Why didn't you return any of my calls? I ended up having to get in touch with Gordon to make sure you were okay."

I didn't understand how Gordon could know I was okay, but I didn't have time to discuss any of that.

"I had my phone off. Did you know one of the residents is missing?"

He furrowed his brow. "No. I worked most of the night and only just got here. I didn't have time to talk to anyone. Which resident is missing?"

I explained that Elsie had dementia and how worried I was about her. "I'm going to go looking for her. When she was assigned to me, she was always heading off in the wrong direction when she went to her room. I think she might be in an unused part of the building. There's lots of old broken equipment lying around. Maybe she tripped over some of it and got hurt."

"You mean like, 'help I've fallen and can't get up?' I'm sure Janet has had people out looking for her." He kissed my forehead and started working his way down my jaw line.

Janet? As in Janet Mulgrew? He's on a first name basis?

I was normally distracted by his kisses, but they had no effect on me then as I thought about the overworked staff and how disinterested they probably were in looking in the creepier sections of the compound. "Mrs. Mulgrew, your Janet, let a few people look in the residents' rooms for Elsie when they first realized she was gone," I glanced around the room and lowered my voice. "But she didn't give them much time or free range, so I doubt they were allowed to look 'everywhere.'"

"What do you mean by 'everywhere'? Just where all have you been?" Frank asked me, pulling back from his kissing with a puzzled look on his face.

"This place has a lot of unused space. I know some of it." I shuddered to think about the cadaver elevator and hoped she hadn't crawled in there. "I didn't go in the basement or the North Wing, but I did search a lot of the older, unused areas when I was looking for a safe place to sleep at night." I gave another shudder thinking about the dark, dank areas that still lay unexplored. I knew I'd have to go there if I couldn't find Elsie in the areas I already knew about.

"I'm going to go search for her. I can't stand the thought of someone who's confused already wandering around in the places I've seen, and especially the places I've *not* seen."

He blew out a breath. "Okay, but you are not going searching alone. If Janet lets you off work to search, I'll cancel my morning appointments and come with you."

I didn't tell him that I wasn't planning on asking permission.

I asked Nikki to keep an eye on my assigned residents, and she said she would—for a price.

I dressed warm, grabbed my flashlight and Frank and I started down the hall where the working girls' sleeping quarters were. He paused at doors to where the immigrants slept, but I knew Elsie couldn't have gotten in there because those doors were always locked. We moved on to the next hallway I'd found. I was glad we didn't linger long in that area; something about it made me uncomfortable.

The darkened hallway wasn't as creepy with Frank at my side. When we searched the old shower area, he saw my makeshift bed on the bench.

"This is where you've been sleeping? This is the safe, secure area you found?" he asked.

I shrugged. "I felt safer here than in an unlocked room with three other girls I don't know and probably wouldn't have gotten to know because they barely speak English."

He made a small growl in his throat before saying, "You are coming back to the hotel with me tonight."

My heart leapt in my chest as I felt a zing go through my body. Too bad I wasn't going to take him up on that offer. "I can't do that," I told him.

"Why not? I'm not letting you stay here. This place gives me the creeps."

I smiled to think I had braved out several nights in a place that gave a tough, undercover FBI agent the creeps.

Score one for me.

"I have to stay here. I'll be okay. I need to stay on-site," I told him. "I'm still trying to get more information from Mr. Anderson, remember?"

"Oh yeah. Him. I tried to talk to him when he came in for his therapy sessions but that jerk Ramon never left his side. I couldn't do much with him hovering over Anderson every second. I'll have to think up a way to get Ramon to leave the area."

We traversed the boarded-up-window hall where I'd first heard the strange noises. Unlike all the other broken doors and dysfunctional windows in this hall, one solid, substantial steel door looked new. I tried the handle. It was locked, but I thought I heard a sound just on the other side of the door. I rapped on the steel door with my fist and then cupped my hand around my ear and pressed it against the door.

"Is that you, Andrew?" a weak, thready voice came from the other side of the door. I tried the knob again, but the door was locked tight.

"Can you open the door on your side?" I shouted at the door.

"No. It won't open."

I told Frank, "It's Elsie. She must have gotten locked inside,"

"Hold on, Elsie," I shouted through the door. "We need to get someone to unlock this door."

"No! No!" she shouted and then began to cry. "You can't do that! Then they'll know I was in here. It will ruin everything. Don't get anyone. Don't leave me in here. Don't leave me alone. Find something to break the lock."

I was amazed at how quickly Frank was able to gain access to the room with only a thin wire to work the lock. Once we were inside, he examined the door's lock.

"This is a deadbolt that requires a key for both entry and exit." He closed the door gently, so the lock didn't re-engage.

We looked around at the tables and counters of what must have been the laboratory when the center was a hospital. The countertops were slate with Bunsen burners hooked up to gas outlets above the lab counters. There were some spilled powders on the countertops, but the area was otherwise free of accumulated dust.

Elsie was cowering behind a gleaming metal contraption that dominated the center of the room. There was a hopper bowl on top and crank handle to the side.

Some sort of test equipment from when the center was a working facility for patients?

"Where is Andrew? It was 'til death do we part.' Where is he?" Elsie screeched at us, her face peering out from behind the hopper thing on top of the machine.

Her gray hair was in wild array. Her clothes filthy. Her eyes, huge as saucers, looked at us before they went wild and staring again.

"Holy Jesus, Mary, Mother of God," said Frank. "How did she get in here?"

Elsie seemed to calm as her gaze went to his. "I got in here when they were bringing in boxes from that noisy rotating submarine. Nobody looking. Too busy watching their feet and the outside. After the stoplights stopped, the people left, but the door was locked, and I couldn't get out to find Andrew, so I laid down to rest until Andrew could come and get me. But, he didn't come. 'Til death do us part.' Where is Andrew?" She began to twirl the band on the ring finger of her left hand around and around, saying over and over, "Andrew."

I whispered to Frank, "She has Alzheimer's. Andrew is her brother."

"Well, let's get her back to her room. She has got to be hungry and cold."

As Frank approached her, Elsie's eyes began to take on a crazed look again as she began backing away from him towards the boxes and crates that were stacked along the walls.

"Don't come near me. I don't know you. You might be one of them. I want Andrew!" She began wedging herself behind some of the stacked boxes, her wide eyes wilder then I'd ever seen them.

I motioned for Frank to back off. "You're scaring her. Let me see if I can get her to come to me." I began a very slow walk towards her, all the while speaking in a calm voice. "I can take you to Andrew. He's been crying for you. He's very upset that you ran away."

"He is?" A pained look scrunched her face. "I didn't run away. Andrew and I were part of this week's scout troop. I just got separated from him when I found this area. I win the prize this week. I found them. Only no one knows I found them because I couldn't report back. I hope they aren't mad at me for not giving my report."

"That's okay. No one is mad. Everything will be all right now. I will take you to Andrew. You remember me don't you?" I was almost to her.

Carefully. Cautiously. Slowly. I stepped forward and reached out my hand to her.

She took it. "Yes. I remember you. The only one who doesn't make fun of us. You're the lady that brings the breakfast trays and fills the pitchers."

"That's right. I'm Genie. I know you're cold and it's been a long time since you've seen your brother so I'd like to take you to him."

A puzzled look crossed her face and was replaced by anger. She yanked her hand out of mine. "You're lying! My brother is dead. He drank the water."

Oh, no. What could I say to get through to her twisted view of the world?

"No. Andrew is alive. I can take you to him. You'll see."

"Andrew's alive? Well, that's good. You must take me to Andrew. I have to warn Andrew not to drink the water."

I shrugged a "she's crazy" at Frank, but he was looking around the room, studying things, carefully stepping around the boxes and counters, with those darn glasses on. He held the frames and squeezed the sides of the frames periodically. After he finished studying the room, he took his glasses off, and his gaze returned to me.

"I'll lock the room back up behind us and let's not say anything to anyone about where we found her, okay?"

"Sure," I said, removing my sweater to drape around Elise's shaking, thin shoulders. "But, there are sure to be questions. Where do we say we found her?"

"I think your little hidey hole in the showers would be a

believable spot, don't you?"

"But if I tell anyone about that, they'll close it off, so no one else gets lost in there. Then where will I sleep tonight?"

He smiled, and the glint in his eye was his only answer.

CHAPTER 19

Grew gave both Frank and me the third degree. She wanted to know where we'd found Elsie, why we'd left our work duties, how long we'd been gone, and what parts of the facility we'd been in. Frank answered most of the questions and skillfully evaded giving details on each item without it seeming to be evasion.

At last, satisfied with his responses, she released us to return to work; but just as I suspected, workers came with boards and nails and sealed up the old shower area, leaving me with little options for the night.

By the time Frank and I pulled into the parking lot of the Ramada Inn I was a jittery wreck and a little surprised at the location. I thought he'd said Grew had him up in the Hampton.

I was so nervous I didn't say anything, not about the change in hotels, not about Frank's sudden sullenness and lack of conversation, and certainly not the way he refused to look at me. My bigamist husband, Jorgji had been standoffish and distant every time he left me to be with his other wife.

I didn't want to think of Frank in that context, but I did it anyway. I couldn't help it. I had caught Frank and Grew in an embrace in her office. I knew what Grew wanted from him.

Every time she looked at him, she couldn't hide her interest.

Does the FBI require their undercover agents to do things like that in the line of duty? Can it be that Frank is avoiding me and becoming moody because he feels guilty about having to play nice later with Grew? Would Frank do something like that?

I thought back to the times Frank and I had been together. There were a few times he had more than ample opportunity to take advantage of my situation but chose not to. My knowledge of the things we'd faced together, what we had been through and what we meant to each other reassured me that he wouldn't do anything to harm our relationship.

Or, at least, I think he wouldn't.

So where does that leave my circumstances and me at that moment? We were in a motel room, but he didn't seem to be interested in making love to me. *Is this going to be another time he'll be a gentleman and not take advantage of my circumstances?* I didn't know if I should get undressed, and try to make the first move to get him into bed with me or not.

Has he really taken me to a motel just to sleep?

Compared to the shower stall bench, that bed at the Ramada was downright luxurious. That night would have been heaven—if Frank had been there with me.

After he took me to retrieve my car from the airport, we went back to the Ramada Inn, where he packed some binoculars, water bottles, snacks and other things in a small travel bag, and left a key card for me on the bedside table, all without much conversation or even eye contact.

I had enough of the tension and his gentlemanly ways and decided to do something about it. I ran to him and stopped him before he could get out the door. He turned to face me and then looked away. I reached up and placed my hand on his cheek to turn his face back to mine.

If he didn't want to be with me, I needed him to say it, so I was sure of how things were. "I don't want you to leave, but I also don't want you to make up a work excuse to leave. If you don't want to be with me tonight, it's okay. Just tell me, and I'll understand."

He smiled at me, took my face in his hands, and kissed me soundly, his arms then drifting down to my shoulders and arms as the kiss deepened. Then he took off, advising me not to wait up for him.

"Wait," I said, grabbing his arm and trying to pull him to me. "Where are you going?"

He let my hand stay on his arm, but he turned his face away. "I have to work tonight."

"Tonight? I thought you'd made that up as an excuse to leave. I thought the day job at the Center was your work?" I was confused about just what he needed to do so badly that would require me to not stay up waiting for him.

****

Frank hadn't wanted to leave Imogene alone in his room. His desire to be with her was so intense he had trouble shaking it and getting down to business, but he had to stay focused. It was a good thing she had been too nervous to pressure him to stay.

He'd avoided looking at her or touching her after they'd returned to his hotel room. He couldn't take a chance on being too close or too intimate with her in any manner, because he knew that would be his undoing. If he felt her soft skin or held her, he knew he'd never want to leave her.

Then, before he left, before he could get out of that room, she'd stopped him, and he'd gone and looked directly at her. When she reached out to him, he couldn't help it. He wanted the memory of her face to take with him.

That had been a mistake. When he'd seen the hurt and confusion his avoidance had on her, he relented and kissed her good-bye. The thought of what was probably going to happen at the rehab center and what he had to do that night began to fade as thoughts of what he wanted to do overtook him. Tasting the sweetness of her lips, feeling the silkiness of her hair, and the softness of her body as she melded herself to him made it worse than torture to pull away. It was a long journey, but his sense of duty finally rose to the surface, and he managed to pull himself away before they landed on the bed together.

He consoled his aching need by telling himself there would be other times with Imogene; she was safe, sleeping in a warm bed in a room he had personally secured and that room was a damn sight better than that spot she had been holed up in at the center.

She continued to amaze him. She had not only secured an undercover job at the center, but she'd also found a secure place to stay every night without anyone finding out about it, had bravely taken off to find that lost woman earlier, and had already gotten some bits and pieces of information from Mr. Andrews. She was resourceful and full of surprises.

Despite his warm thoughts of Imogene, Frank's legs began to ache from the cold. When they started cramping, he set the binoculars down and stood up from the frozen ground for a bit, stamping his feet and waving his arms to generate some heat.

He wished he'd had time to get John Gringer there for some assistance. It was easier doing surveillance with a buddy to spell you, and John was the best. But when Frank got into the room where Elsie had hidden and saw those boxes packed and ready for shipment, he knew this was the operation he been sent to this location to investigate, and if he didn't do surveillance that night, the evidence he needed could be out the door before John ever got there.

John had asked for another agent to spell him at the foreign port of entry in Chicago, where the illegal cargo was entering from China, and said he would get to the center as soon as he could. In the meantime, Frank was on his own. There were no other FBI agents in the area, and he wasn't authorized to work with any of the locals since they didn't know who was involved in this operation or who might have been compromised. That meant Frank would have to cover the entire night's surveillance without a break.

When Frank began to get drowsy he slapped his face and pinched his sides; the pain helped wake him up. He was assured he hadn't missed any activity that might have gone on at the back entrance to the rehab center.

****

I ended up going to bed, in my sleep shorts and the Detroit Tiger's tee shirt that had once been Frank's. The bed was comfortable, and given my emotional and physical exhaustion from the tension of the day, it wasn't hard to drift off to sleep thinking pleasant thoughts surrounding Frank's recent kisses.

Sometime around early morning, a heavy blackness overcame my dreams and I began to sleep fitfully, despite the comfort of the bed.

Just before 4 o'clock, I awoke with a fright. The room was still, and only a sliver of light from the parking lot came in through the crack in the curtains. I tried to calm down and stop freaking out; even in my groggy state, I knew it was the dream that had me on edge—not anything going on in the room.

I'd been dreaming of the dark. At six years of age, I had been old enough and wise enough to not fall for any of Martin's tricks, but he had put the tin heart from my birthday wand in a chest in their family's attic. That heart was all that was left of the last gift I'd received from my parents. I had to get it back, but I was too frightened to go to the attic alone. I tried to talk Mandy into going with me, but she refused. Instead, she made Martin go with me to the attic, ostensibly to keep me from being afraid.

The stacks of papers and clothing piled around the chest should have been a clue of what he and Mandy had planned for me, but when Martin opened the chest, all I could see was the heart from the top of my wand inside and I instinctively reached for it.

The chest was deep, and I was off balanced and unprepared for Martin's push. I fell into the depths of the trunk, just barely managing to keep from banging my head against the sides of the almost empty space. Martin slammed the heavy lid down, and my world turned to black. It was several suffocating, terror-filled minutes before Mandy came to release me from the trunk.

The inside of that trunk was the blackness I saw in my dream. The darkness was all around me, and I couldn't get out of it because I was locked inside. I felt helpless and powerless. Trapped.

Was that how Frank had felt when the water had risen over his head in Chicago's deep tunnel? Is he out in the night facing danger again?

As much as I hoped Frank was safe wherever he was, whatever he was doing, I didn't dare call him to reassure myself he was okay. He had told me to not wait up, and I think that implied he was going to be gone the entire night.

I dredged up my many years of therapy to calm myself enough to sleep. When I found I couldn't sleep in the dark, I got up and turned on the bathroom light and left the door open a crack, so it lit the room.

Frank still hadn't come back to the room when the bedside alarm rang a few hours later. Disappointed at showering alone, but grateful I'd made it through the night without a complete breakdown and thankful for the hot water, I lingered in the shower longer than strictly necessary. As the water rained down on my body, I relaxed and began to think more clearly about my dilemma with Frank.

Why did Frank leave me alone all night? Was it really work? What kind of work? Does it involve Grew?

I conjured up visions of Frank leaving me to meet Grew at the Hampton Inn where she had arranged for him to stay because, as Mazie put it, Grew had the hots for Frank. Then I remembered that all of Frank's things were here at the Ramada, and not at the Hampton; I shook off my jealousy and got dressed for work.

Careful not to get lost, I drove to the Center with my car. If Frank already knew I was at the center, there was no need to hide my car anymore.

Mazie fired all types of questions at me the second I brought in her breakfast tray.

"Rumor has it that you and that hunky physical therapist have the hots for each other and that you were looking for a secluded spot to do the deed when you found Elsie hiding in one of the older parts of the building."

"We were not looking for a spot to do 'the deed.' We were looking for Elsie!" I pulled the lid off her plate. Eggs and soggy toast again.

"Well. You don't deny you have the hots for each other. Remember, I saw him hug you in the P.T. room, and someone said they saw you two drive off together last night so you can't deny that."

I could feel my face growing hot under her piercing gaze. "Mr. Buchanan was just being nice. He gave me a ride to my car." I lied again.

"Sure. That's believable. Well, I'm glad someone is having a good time. I called my doctor and told him to cancel my whirlpool therapy. Wasn't any fun. That fella you've got the hots for is all rugged and masculine looking, but he shook like a leaf helping me into the whirlpool and had the nerve to make me get out of it on my own."

That puzzled me. *Was Frank ill?* He had a case of the shakes by the pond, too. *Had his preoccupation last night just been a sign of illness and not a rejection of me?*

When things slowed down, I went to the therapy room. I had to talk to Frank and find out what was going on with him. I found him busy with Mr. Anderson, under the watchful eye of Ramon.

If Frank was ever going to get information out of Mr. Anderson, I had to get Ramon away from that therapy session.

Frank looked up at me when I entered. His smile lit up the entire room and made his dark circled eyes beneath the heavy-rimmed glasses seem less tired. That told me all I needed to know about last night. Frank had not been with Grew.

Or had he? His cheeks were red with slap marks on them. *Had they fought? Or is that her manner of foreplay?*

"Is there something I can help you with?" Frank asked me.

"No. I came here looking for Ramon," I lied. Well, not exactly a lie. I was playing a hunch.

I was pleased that my comment wiped the smile off Frank's face as he darted a look at Ramon, who was so close to the treatment table he might as well have been on it.

Ramon looked up at me. "Can it wait? I'm not supposed to leave Mr. Anderson's side until the relief nurse gets here."

"Ahh. No. It can't." I had no idea of what ruse I was going to use to get Ramon out of that room. I'd have to make something up as I went along.

Ramon hesitated in his response. He was not going to waiver on his duties, so I needed to give him more incentive to leave Mr. Anderson alone.

What could I do to convince him to leave Mr. Anderson in Frank's care?

I leaned my back suggestively against the doorjamb, tilted my head, fluffed my hair, puffed out my chest, and picked up one foot to brace it behind me in what I had hoped was a sexy come-hither look. Too bad I almost missed the door casing entirely, and spun off to the side when I lost my balance.

Stumbling backward in the doorway, I caught myself by grasping at anything for purchase.

Both Frank and Ramon jumped forward as though they thought they would be close enough to stay my fall.

When I latched on to the doorframe and regained my balance, Frank stopped his forward momentum, and the corners of his mouth turned up slightly.

Ramon, however, was all rescuer. Even though I had my balance back, I let him take hold of my elbow to steady me, as I lead him skillfully out into the hallway without him noticing we were leaving the room.

"What is it that you needed to see me about?" he asked.

"I feel a little dizzy. Can you help me get back to the nurses' station?" I put a hand to my head and leaned forward as though I was going to pass out, something I did a lot of, so I knew how to fake it.

"Sure," he said and yelled over his shoulder to Frank, "I'll be right back."

"No rush," said Frank. "Mr. Anderson and I have a lot more to work on in this session."

I didn't like that Ramon had his arm tightly around my waist, but I found it hard to protest, given that I'd told him I was faint. He had a sickly sweet, smoky smell about him that was making me nauseous. Not any cigarette smell I knew of, and I doubted that smell came from an e-cigarette.

Fortunately, no one was at the nurses' station when we got there, so I was able to sit down and remove myself from Ramon's uncomfortable embrace.

"So what did you need to see me about?" he asked.

Oh, darn. I needed to come up with something fast.

"I know that you and Nikki sometimes go outside for a quick smoke."

He looked around and shushed me. "Hey. Keep that to yourself. I'm not supposed to leave Mr. Anderson's side. It's just that sometimes he's asleep and I figure a minute or two away won't hurt anything."

"I'm not concerned with your leaving him. I just want to know if you saw anything suspicious that day when I stumbled across Pricilla's body. Or if you've noticed anyone hanging around outside the building since."

"Is that what you pulled me away from P.T. for? To ask if I noticed anything on my smoke breaks?"

Had I given Frank enough time to question Mr. Anderson?

I didn't think so. Frank probably needed more time, so I blinked my eyes, trying to make them bat like Mandy did.

"You get something in your eye?"

Frustrated, I said, "No. I'm trying to flirt with you."

"You are?" Ramon smiled and showed a small chin dimple and a row of straight, white teeth. "That's cute. And, flattering. Rumor has it you are into that P.T. guy. They said you left together last night."

Wow. Rumors get around fast.

"He gave me a ride to my car. We didn't spend the night together." *Not that I didn't want to.*

Ramon's smile widened. "I've got to get back to Mr. Anderson. Why don't I come to the sleeping quarters for the ladies tonight after your shift, and we can spend some time together." He winked, turned away, and started walking back to Frank and Mr. Anderson.

In a panic, I ran after him and grabbed his arm. He turned around, and I planted a big kiss on his lips. He grabbed me around the waist and returned the kiss, trying to get some tongue action included. I had no choice but to keep my lips pressed together and let the kiss continue for an appropriate length of time before I pulled away.

"Why don't we meet at the little gazebo by the pond," I said. "You know, the one where you go to smoke. It'll be the beginning of shift so no one will be there that early and we can have the place to ourselves."

He grinned a wicked grin. "You are one smart cookie. I like the idea of making love in a gazebo. I'll bring a blanket— although, you're so hot we may not need it."

He grabbed me and his head came towards mine again.

I gave him a playful shove and told him, "Save something for tonight."

****

Frank knew it was no good to be impatient with Mr. Anderson, who was doing his best. It helped that the glasses Frank wore had video feedback to headquarters where a real physical therapist was watching and coaching Frank every step of the way. Mr. Anderson seemed eager to get some information out, but his aphasia prevented verbal communication. He was writing another note in response to Frank's asking if he had some idea of who the double agent was.

It was slow going as Mr. Anderson laboriously made each letter of the name. Ramon came in before the last two letters of the name were done, but Frank didn't need to know the last letters, he'd seen enough.

What he saw made his gut churn, and he wondered what he should do with the information that he now had at his fingertips.

****

By the time I left Ramon, Rorry was clanging his bedrails, and everyone else needed my attention. I had to wait until my break before I could get back to the therapy room. I was so eager to learn what Frank had discovered that I left for my break a few minutes early. When I got to the P.T. room, the door was closed and locked.

I was sick to see the sign that said P.T. was canceled due to the illness of the therapist.

Is this my confirmation that Frank is ill?

Worried, I pulled out my cell and began dialing his number. He didn't answer the first call, so I kept calling non-stop, and on the seventh call, he finally answered.

"I can't talk to you right now Imogene. I'm driving."

Driving?

"You're leaving? Why?" And, then my heart leaped in my chest with excitement. "You learned something, didn't you? It has to be big if you left right away."

Was the news so important he couldn't even take the time to let me know he was leaving?

"Uhh, I didn't learn much, but what I did learn requires that I go talk with someone before I do anything else."

"Talk with someone? Why couldn't you talk to me? I helped. This is my investigation. I started it."

"I'm so sorry. I can't talk to you until after I meet with someone involved in the case." He said another weak, feeble, "I'm sorry," and then disconnected the call.

Calling back was not an option. If he didn't want to talk to me, then I didn't want to talk to him. Besides, I still had a job to do. That paycheck I'd gotten was the first real money I'd ever made, and I didn't want to lose my job as a nurse's aide. At least not until I bought a few more skeins of yarn that I'd been yearning for.

CHAPTER 20

Gordon met Frank at the halfway point. The truck stop was crowded and noisy, but that was all the better for their conversation to stay private.

"How's Imogene?" were the first words out of Gordon's mouth after the waitress sat down their coffee and left them alone.

"You know about her getting the job at the rehab?"

Gordon smiled. "I have a remote feed on the security system. It was pretty obvious when she left. I was able to monitor various points in the house and knew she hadn't been there. Her telling me she had a cake in the oven confirmed it. Imogene can't cook."

"How'd you discover she got a job at the center to get access to Mr. Anderson?"

"I didn't know for sure. I only knew she wasn't at the house. You just confirmed where she was."

Frank wanted to slap himself, and not because he was tired. Gordon had just used the oldest trick in the book to get information and Frank had fallen for it.

"Don't beat yourself up for letting the cat out of the bag. It was a pretty easy deduction that she'd have gone there. I'm actually very proud of her being able to pull off that level of subterfuge. It's like she's a chip off the old block. She would make a good secret agent."

Frank's face twisted in agony at those words. "You may just be right about her being a chip off the old block."

No sense in delaying what he'd come there to do. Frank pulled two slips of paper out of his pocket. One of them he shoved across the table to Gordon.

Gordon looked at the words 'She is a Ru' and said nothing. Frank studied Gordon's face carefully before shoving the second paper across the table to him.

There in pencil were the words, 'Kathleen Warr'.

Gordon's face darkened. "What are these? Who wrote them?"

"Given where I just came from, I am pretty sure you can guess who wrote them."

"David Anderson?"

Frank nodded.

Gordon rubbed a hand over his face as a heavy shock and fatigue set in. He'd worked so long on trying to find the double agent who had set him up. Now that he had the information, it was plain and obvious as the black coffee that sat untouched in front of him.

"Good God. Does Imogene know?"

"She saw the note that implied the spy was Russian but she didn't seem to understand the significance of it. She was just elated that the note inferred the spy was a 'she' and not a 'he.'"

"She didn't see the second note?" Gordon asked with urgency in his voice.

"No. I high-tailed it out of there straight to you. What do you want me to do with this information?" Frank asked.

Gordon seemed not to hear the question. His eyes stared blankly out the window at the approaching blackness of night. After one long bout of silence, he turned to face Frank and said in a low, calm voice that Frank had to strain to hear, "All these years. Never suspecting. Never knowing."

Frank asked again, "What do you want me to do with this information? It isn't part of my FBI assignment, or why I'm at the Center, so I'm not obligated to report it. That's why I wanted to come to you first. It's up to you what I do with it."

Gordon stirred his untouched coffee while he mulled this new revelation over for a bit.

Gordon knew with this information, he could easily be cleared of the charges he faced. He could build a strong case against the spy. He had plenty of evidence now that the dots had been connected.

He also knew he'd be destroying two people he loved in the process. One may have only been a memory, but the other was alive and finally just starting her life, just beginning to come out of her shell and experience the world. This would be devastating.

Gordon shoved the papers back across the table to Frank.

"Destroy these. Tell no one what you've learned."

Frank let out the breath he'd been holding in, relief washing over him. "You sure? If the truth doesn't come out, you'll be eternally a hunted man. You can never resume your former life; you'll be forever labeled a traitor."

"I'll take being labeled a traitor if it means Imogene never finding out that her mother was one."

CHAPTER 21

Frank had reluctantly returned to the P.T. department at the center. As much as he wanted to find Genie and take her away with him, his undercover job at this facility was far from over. The contraband had not been moved in the night as he'd expected. John Gringer was now outside keeping an eye on the exterior of the building. There was much Frank had to do undercover, on the inside of this ever-expanding FBI case.

He knew ICE was investigating the center for employing illegal aliens, but the criminal activities going on at the center went far beyond that, as their monitoring of the shipments at the harbor was already proving.

As a professional courtesy, Frank normally would have notified the ICE undercover agent Ramon Sanchez that he was at the center doing an FBI investigation, But Frank had been told to trust no one on the inside, and his gut instinct had backed that up.

The foreign girls working at the center were being funneled in by someone, and Frank didn't put it past another agency's employee to be involved, so he kept his mouth shut and his eyes open.

Now, not only was he worried about Genie being in the

middle of an immigration sting, and an FBI investigation, he was worried about this new bit of information from Anderson. You couldn't add fuel to an already lit fire and expect it to be extinguished. What was he going to do about Genie?

****

Frank was alone in the P.T. room at his desk when I walked in. He was reading something, or rather, just staring at two pieces of paper on the desk in front of him.

When he saw me, he folded the papers and slipped them into his pocket.

His embrace was warm but loose and controlled. I was shut out again.

"Have you talked to who you wanted to talk to? Are you now able to tell me about the information you found?"

He shook his head, "I don't think so."

"Which 'I don't think so'? You don't think you can talked to the right person or you don't think you are able to tell me what's going on?"

He drew me in close to his chest. His hand stroked my hair, and he pressed my cheek against him. His breathing was even and slow, but I could feel his heart pounding rapidly in his chest.

"The only thing I can tell you is you need to go home now. There is no longer a need for you to stay here."

"You got the name of the double spy and can clear my father?" *If that was the case then why was he so melancholy?*

"No."

I looked up at him, searching for a crack in the armor. "Which 'no' are you referring to? No, you didn't get the name of the..."

"Just no." He stiffened and released me as Nikki wheeled Rorry into the room in a wheelchair. He was in his black robe, hanging onto a set of crutches he balanced on his lap.

Frank scowled at Nikki. "Why isn't he dressed and why is he in a wheelchair? He is supposed to be using his crutches all the time now." The anger in his voice seemed to be more than necessary for the circumstances with Rorry.

Something had Frank on edge.

Nikki shrugged. "He never gets dressed and didn't want to use the crutches. Told me to get him a wheelchair."

Frank set his jaw, picked up his heavy glasses and put them on before going to set the brakes on the wheelchair so Rorry could get out of it.

Rorry hopped up and swung his crutches up and around before he got them easily under his control.

I pitied Rorry. I wouldn't have wanted to be on the receiving end of the smolder Frank was giving him. I quietly ducked out of the room, intending to find Frank later and get to the bottom of what was going on—for my father's sake.

As usual, my shift was over before I knew it. Twelve-hour days were exhausting, but that didn't account for the dragging of my feet as I grabbed my coat. I felt guilty over leaving Ramon waiting at the gazebo for me when I had no intentions of a rendezvous with him.

Frank was getting some shut-eye stretched out on one of the therapy benches in the P.T. room, because he was planning on 'working' again tonight and had told me to go home.

I knew he meant I should go back to Winnetka but I wasn't going to go home. I still had the motel key card Frank had given me in my pocket. I let him think I was going home and didn't tell him I was leaving for the motel alone.

I was uncomfortable with deceiving Frank, but what could I do? He had a dangerous, undercover job to do and I was determined to not be one of those women who resent their man spending time at work. I was determined to prove Janey wrong about her assumptions about us. Frank and I could make a relationship work. I would not be the clinging vine she thought I was.

Except, there had already been one murder that I knew of and I was worried about Frank. I also had to tell Ramon I wasn't going to have sex with him and didn't know how he would take that rejection so I wanted someone to know where I had gone, just in case I disappeared like some of the others.

I went down the hall and lightly knocked on the P.T. door. It opened right away.

"Good. I didn't wake you."

"No. I'm getting ready for my nighttime duties. Why haven't you left already?"

"I'm going, but before I can leave this place, I have to go to the gazebo by the pond to let Ramon know I'm not going to meet with him tonight. I wanted someone to be aware of my whereabouts—just in case he didn't take the news well."

Frank arched an eyebrow, but only said, "Take your time, but if you're not back here in 5 minutes, I'm going to come and get you."

"Deal," I said.

Ramon wasn't in the gazebo. I should have been elated that I didn't have to face him, but instead, I was offended.

He stood me up. The nerve of the man.

It was cold, and I was shivering when I stepped out of the gazebo to go back into the building, intending to let Frank know I was okay before leaving for the motel.

I took a quick look around, just to be sure Ramon wasn't delayed and still on his way to the gazebo.

That's when I saw a green-uniformed body out in the middle of the frozen pond.

It was Ramon.

CHAPTER 22

Frank and I almost collided as I dashed back into the building just as he was coming out to check on me.

He sensed my panic immediately and seized my shoulders to steady me. "What is it?"

"Come quick! It's Ramon. He's out on the pond. He's not moving. I think he might be dead!"

Breathless, I pulled away and raced back to the pond. Once at the pond, I took a tentative step out onto the ice, fearful it might not hold, and I'd be plunged into the icy water just beneath the surface.

I was almost to Ramon when I became aware that Frank was not behind me. He stood on the rim of the pond, one foot almost touching the ice sheet that covered the water.

In the moonlight, I saw the look on Frank's face. I knew that look and knew it well. I'd worn that look before and began to have an idea of what was causing it.

I heard a small 'cracking' sound in the ice beneath my feet and knew the ice was going to give way beneath Ramon's heavier weight if I didn't get him moved. I had no time to waste.

"Don't come out!" I shouted back to Frank. "The ice is too

thin for both our weight. I'm going to try to slide him over to you."

I didn't waste time looking to see if Frank was following my orders. I stretched myself out flat on the ice and grabbed Ramon's pant leg and tugged. The warmth of his body must have melted a thin layer of ice and made the surface slippery, because his body slid along without much effort as I wriggled, shoved, pulled, and skated him over to the edge of the pond.

Frank grabbed hold of his shirt and pulled him to shore, then stepped away from the pond.

Wet and shivering, I bent over Ramon. He didn't appear to be breathing. I checked for a pulse. It was weak. I could still detect no breathing, so I sealed his nose, covered his mouth with mine and began rescue breathing.

Ramon, unconscious and unresponsive, was rushed by ambulance to the local hospital, where we learned he died of a drug overdose without ever regaining consciousness.

That was one too many deaths for me to handle, so I gave Grew my two-week's notice.

Frank was livid when I told him.

"I thought you told me I should go home?" I said. "Now you're upset that I am following your wishes?"

"I thought you were going last night. I want you to leave now, immediately. Right this minute. Not wait two weeks." He was pacing the floor of the P.T. room, brushing his hands over his hair, the glasses discarded on the desk.

"How can I do that? We're already short staffed here as it is. It's Christmas Day. Who's going to take care of the residents?"

Now that Frank had said he had the information he needed from Mr. Anderson, I didn't understand why he was staying at the center. I was reluctant to leave with him still there. Besides, I had gifts to give my people and the cat.

"You are driving me crazy!" Frank told me. "I have to continue my work here. I can't be worried about your safety every minute. You have to go home."

"I'm not asking you to worry about me. My taekwondo instructor says I'm learning some of the basic moves; I just need to not be so timid. So see, I can sort of take care of myself."

"Beginning taekwondo is nothing compared to what you might be facing here. You need to go home, NOW!"

I'd never seen this level of anger with Frank before, not even with Rorry.

"I'll go home tonight, after Christmas presents are opened. I can't leave before Christmas is over. I made things for my people."

He huffed, but seemed mollified. "Okay. I can see the logic in that, but after the gift giving you need to leave, pronto."

"I'll think about it," was all I would commit to.

I thought for once the kitchen might prepare a decent meal for Christmas, but I'd been wrong. The table was set with spam shaped like a turkey, instant mashed potatoes, and canned mixed veggies.

After dinner, the residents all gathered around the Christmas tree in the lobby to sing carols and open presents.

Mr. George smiled widely when he opened the fluffy green slippers I'd made him, complete with a frog on top of each one.

"As a boy, I used to collect tadpoles and then let 'em go when they were frogs. These are great. Thank you, Genie."

Everyone else seemed pleased with the animal themed slippers I handed them. Mazie chuckled over the monkey ones I gave her. When Mrs. Jones opened her gift and saw not only a pair of giraffe slippers but a jiggle ball toy for her cat she smiled and tucked the toy in her pocket.

The last package I'd brought was intended for Ramon. When I saw his name on the tag I'd place on the teddy bear slippers, I started to cry at the thought he'd never wear them.

All the residents gathered around to console me. Each gave me a sugar cookie that they'd carefully wrapped in paper napkins and tied with yarn bows, all saved from earlier in the day. I couldn't help but smile and feel better, warmed by their generosity and affection.

Christmas evening was drawing to a close and I was going to get my coat when Mrs. Jones came running down the hall towards me, the fluffy cat in her arms jostling with each pounding step she took. Zina Flowers followed close behind them.

"Please, Miss Genie, help my cat."

The cat looked up at me, wide-eyed. I petted the cat, and it began to purr.

"She's going to die," Mrs. Jones wailed, hugging the cat to her chest. He wriggled and squirmed, but Mrs. Jones held him tight in her arms.

From what I could see, the cat seemed annoyed that she couldn't get down, and she was far from death's door. I pulled Mrs. Jones off into a side conference room before anyone could spy the struggling cat. Zina followed us in, her head down; her face a frown.

"Why don't you sit down and tell me what this is all about," I said to the ladies, expecting the story to have something to do with the grim reaper Zina always thought she saw in her room.

They both began to talk at once.

"She was in my room...."

"She came into my room..."

"One at a time please," I said. "You go first, Mrs. Jones."

Zina glanced furtively around the room and began wringing her hands together while Mrs. Jones told me, "It's freezing cold outside, so I brought Tickles inside."

"Tickles?" I asked.

"Yes." She held up her cat who let his legs dangle limply before struggling to get down. "I call her Tickles because she likes to be tickled on her belly. Anyway. I had her in my room with me last night. When I got up this morning, she was gone."

Here Zina took over the story. "Tickles had come into my room. When I woke up this morning, I saw her at my night side stand eating the pills I'd been hiding there."

"She ate your valium?" I asked trying to remember how many pills I had seen in that drawer.

"There was only one left when I pulled her away and ran to get Jones," Zina explained.

"So we have to get her stomach pumped," said Mrs. Jones who had finally sat down in a chair. "She's been poisoned by those pills. That many will kill her for sure."

I agreed that if she'd consumed all the pills that Zina had been accumulating, she should be dead or at least heavily sedated. I picked up the fluffy cat with the orange, white, and brown markings and stared into her enormous eyes.

The pupils were slits. *Was that normal for a cat?* She gave a small 'meow' and struggled to remove herself from my grasp. I handed her back to Mrs. Jones.

What was I to do? Cats weren't supposed to be in the building. Grew would not be sympathetic to Zina hoarding her pills or Mrs. Jones hiding a cat in her room.

Tickles gave me the answer when she purred, rolled over and waited for her usually tummy rub.

"How long ago did she eat the pills?"

They both looked at each other and then at the clock on the wall.

"It's been 15 minutes since I found her crunching on the pills," said Zina.

"That's long enough that she should be showing some effects of the pills. She seems fine to me."

They both looked at the cat, which was now flipped back over on all fours and head bumping Mrs. Jones's hand wanting to get her attention. Purring loudly.

Having reassured them both the cat was okay, I went into Zina's room and pocketed the lone pill from her nightstand so I could give it to Melton to have it analyzed.

CHAPTER 23

I pulled on a thick pair of socks, my boots, and gloves. The parka came last before I picked up my suitcase and headed out to the parking lot to my car.

I was angry with Frank for making me agree to head directly back to Gordon's apartment. It wasn't really fair that he had this measure of control over me. I hated it when he begged. It was undignified for an FBI agent to beg—and it always got me to cave in.

I'd given him the black knit hat I'd made for him and disgruntledly wished him a Merry Christmas before grumpily heading to get my things and go to my car. His insistence I leave had put a damper on Christmas.

After being parked for 12 hours in a shower of freezing rain, the car was coated in ice so thick I couldn't get the door unlocked. I chipped away at the ice around the door lock and then put the key in my mouth to warm it, hoping that if I put a warm key in the lock, it might thaw the ice enough to allow me to unlock my door.

I was anxious as I worked on the lock. The parking area was pitch black. The lights that were supposed to illuminate the area were either turned off or burned out. Knowing Grew, they were probably turned off as a cost savings measure. After all, most of the staff lived on site, and except Mazie, none of the residents could come and go. There were very few cars in the lot and while I was adequately clothed, I was shaking with an overwhelming fear of the dark and the isolation.

Frank was somewhere out there in the dark with his nighttime binoculars, but that gave me no comfort. He wasn't there in the dark to keep an eye on me; it was whatever was going on at the center that had his attention. He was probably closer to the North Wing, where we'd found Elsie, of no use to me in this parking lot.

I set my resolve. I had to get that ice cleared away. As I continued to focus on getting into my locked car, I thought about all the things I knew about the center, and its inhabitants.

Rorry is better, but doesn't want to be, why else would he refuse to get dressed or use his crutches? Zina isn't helped by the pills she's given even when she takes them. Rose is the only one of the West Wing staff allowed to work in the East Wing, and everyone else who works the West Wing seems frightened out of their wits if anyone so much as looked at them. Why is that? Do the colored lights have anything to do with it? Are they afraid of ghosts? Is that why they're the only workers given sleeping quarters with locks on the doors?

As I worked on the door lock, I heard a rumbling far off in the distance. I panicked as the *whamp, whamp, whamp* noise grew louder and louder until it was almost over me.

There were those different colored lights in the sky strobing and coming closer to the parking lot. I ducked down just as a helicopter passed over my car, heading towards the North side of the building.

CHAPTER 24

Frank and John Gringer were off at the edge of the woods watching, from their vantage point, the operation occurring in the back of the center. The night-vision binoculars revealed two men loading boxes into the cargo hold of the newly arrived chopper while another man with a gun stood watch.

"Think we've got enough for a strong court case?" John asked Frank.

"I think given the pictures I have from the inside of the production room and the search warrant in my pocket, we can call in the swat team now and get this over with."

"You worried this will mess up the ICE investigation of the illegals they've got going on?"

"Probably, and I suspect ICE will be mad as hell that we get the collar on this operation before they get theirs. But, it can't be helped. From what I can tell this operation and the employment of illegals are linked together, so it isn't possible to separate the ICE part out from our investigation."

"Okay." John picked up his phone and began to text the swat team waiting a mile away on the other side of the woods at the edge of the property.

Frank pulled out his binoculars to count the number of

boxes on the ground that the men were loading.

"Wait," Frank put out his hand and moved John's cell down. "There's a problem."

"What's that?" John asked looking at the lone figure in a parka running towards the back of the building where the helicopter had landed. The person got within 50 feet of the loading, stopped, and hid behind a tree.

Frank groaned. "She's supposed to be on her way home."

Imogene's red parka stood out like a beacon as she drew closer to the men loading boxes into the chopper. Fortunately, no one had bothered to look in her direction. Yet.

"That the woman you're crazy about?" asked John.

"Crazy is an apt description. Cover me," Frank told John. "I've got to get her out of there before she gets killed."

"Want me to hold off on the swat team then?"

"Yeah. Give me a few minutes. It wouldn't do to have her in the crossfire."

"Sure thing. It looks like the loading will take a bit more time so I can give you five. After that, we'll have to get back-up in here, or risk everything going sour."

CHAPTER 25

I could sense someone was approaching me from my right side, but I couldn't see whom in the darkness of the trees. It was just a feeling I had, and I wasn't inclined to ignore that feeling.

I spread my feet shoulder width apart, bent slightly at the knees and pulled my fists up in a defensive posture with my arms ready to block any blows that might come at me; just as I'd been taught by my Taekwondo sensei.

Muscles loose. Head swiveling to survey my environment. Ears tuned to any noise I could hear, I turned to face my attacker, heart thudding, adrenaline surging.

It was Frank.

I let out a whoosh of air, lowered my fists, and relaxed just a tiny bit, but my heart still was beating hard. Frank was who I'd come to find. I only hoped I'd have time to explain what I'd just pieced together while I was trying to get into my locked car.

That helicopter at the back loading area told me there was no time to waste and I wasn't certain Frank knew about the girls and the significance of double deadbolt key-locked doors.

Frank was pulling me back to the safety of the trees when I began to struggle against him.

"You don't understand. They are going to take them."

"We know. We have a swat team coming for the illegal drug runners and their cargo."

"No. Not just the illegal drugs. The girls! You've got to protect the girls." I was perhaps too loud in trying to make him understand, but Rose and the others deserved a chance at freedom. If the helicopter took them away, it would be difficult to find them again and liberate them.

I tried to quickly explain what I'd finally realized, but I was already too late. As I spoke, the immigrant workers were being led out of the building, their thin cotton uniforms no protection from the harsh wind and freezing rain. Heads down, arms around their torsos they staggered under the sudden onslaught of freezing rain as Mark, their boss, herded them out of the building.

Watching them leave, my heart heavy, I felt the muzzle of a gun pressed against my temple, and when I saw the look of horror on Frank's face, I knew it was I who'd distracted him and given our position away. He had been caught off guard. I was sick at what I'd caused.

Once this man with the gun killed me, I knew Frank was next.

CHAPTER 26

I twisted and jerked my arm up rapidly all the while expecting to feel the gun discharge into my temple. The gunman, used to the crowded girls they trafficked, must not have expected me to respond defensively, so he was the one caught off guard this time.

His gun arm flew up, but unfortunately that gun was still clutched in his hand.

Frank wasted no time as he tackled the man, before he had a chance to know what hit him and re-aim. They fell together to the ground, struggling for control of the gun.

The sound of them falling alerted the two men loading the cargo. When they became aware of our presence, they pulled two more guns and took aim directly at me.

Then, pandemonium broke loose. The Center's East Wing residents flowed out of the building towards the men with the guns next to the helicopter. At the same time, an FBI SWAT van careened up the drive towards the back of the center.

By the time the van got to the back area where we were, the men with the guns still had their weapons out but hadn't used them. They were cowering under the onslaught of little old ladies and men, screaming at them and clubbing them with fists, canes, and walkers.

Mark roared at the men fending off the elderly residents. "We've got to get out of here! What are you waiting for? Those people can barely walk. They can't hurt you. Shoot them!"

One of the loading men said, "There're just old people. We can't shoot old people."

Frank was still struggling with his armed assailant, and I was rushing towards the helicopter to get the girls out of it when I heard Mark say, "If you can't do it, I will."

I turned to see Mark wrest one of the guns away from the man who had refused to shoot unarmed old people.

I was torn, but the SWAT members were still some distance away. The gun Mark now had was the more immediate threat. I altered course and raced in his direction as fast as my feet would carry me.

I had only been a short distance away, so just as Mark aimed the gun at Mazie's head my right leg shot out in a roundhouse kick that snapped the weapon from his hand, breaking it in the process. The hand. Not the gun. The gun was picked up by Mazie, who had no trouble aiming it at Mark.

"Call your dogs off, or I'll put a bullet in your head." Then she lowered the gun down to his crotch. "Or other parts that might be more sensitive."

The man instinctively dropped his unbroken hand to cover his unprotected area. "Julio, Tommy, Dean, hold up! Drop your weapons."

The men looked around at all the SWAT team members surrounding them, rifles out and aimed, the elderly patients waiving canes and walkers and shouting at them, and then they looked to Mark, groveling and asking Mazie to not shoot him. Their guns fell as their hands rose.

Frank rushed to take the gun from Mazie's hand before rushing to my side. His partner was already rounding up the helicopter pilot. Several men in flak jackets and body armor gear began converging on the area.

"Imogene! You okay?" Frank asked me, not taking his

eyes or the gun off Mr. Human Trafficker to look at me.

"My foot hurts a little, but I feel great!"

And I did.

People were swirling around Frank and me. The ladies from the West Wing were crying, talking and hugging each other. The residents were all high fiving each other and the guys in the flak jackets were disarming and handcuffing the struggling gunmen.

And, I'd done it. I had managed to execute a perfect roundhouse kick. My sensei had told me I was too kind when I sparred with others and that kindness kept me from perfecting my fighting techniques. He said I needed more focus. More motivation.

He was going to be so proud of me.

CHAPTER 27

Frank gave the gun he'd taken from the loading man to one of the flak jackets and pulled me along out of the fray.

I looked around and saw the man who must have been Frank's surveillance partner walk up to us. He put out his hand to shake mine.

"Wow. That was a rush. I've never seen old people do anything like that. And your kick was the bomb. I'm John Ginger, and you must be Frank's Genie."

"I am," I said, shaking John's hand, please at his denoting me as 'Frank's' Genie.

Then John slapped Frank on the back, laughing. "Frank my man. You are the craziest I've ever seen you, for sure."

Frank smiled, and looked directly into my eyes as he told John, "Totally and irrevocably crazy."

John, still grinning, said, "I wish you luck, man. Looks like your gonna need it. If you can tear yourself away from your main action, we need to clear up the loose ends in the building. You coming?"

Frank looked towards the building, then turned back to me, and said, "John and I need to see if we can find Mulgrew to give her the search warrant and arrest her. I don't suppose it would do any good to tell you to stay here?"

I looked around at the order from chaos the flak jackets were making. "Not a chance. This is the best adrenaline buzz I've ever had. Grew's arrest will be the icing on the cake, and I'm not going to miss that for all the cookies in China."

"Well then," Frank motioned for one of the flak jacket guys to come over. After a brief talk, he took the guy's vest and draped it over my shoulders. It came well below my waist and was so extremely heavy my knees almost buckled from the sudden weight of it.

"Grew has probably taken off and is long gone because people like her always have an escape plan in place. They know this type of thing is bound to happen eventually and get out. But just in case she hasn't left, stay well behind us, and take off at the first sign of trouble or if shots are fired," Frank told me as he, John and I headed into the building.

CHAPTER 28

There was so much commotion outside in the loading area that I hadn't noticed that two East Wing residents had not been in the fray. Mr. George and Mr. Jake were in Grew's office when we got there. It had been their assignment to go to her office to get evidence of her illegal doings.

When the two men found her with her coat on and a box of papers in her hands preparing to flee the building, they stopped her and held her at bay with her letter opener from her desk.

I did as I was instructed by FBI Agent Frank Bauchman and stayed back in the far corner of Grew's office so I could watch him work. Mr. George and Mr. Jake had been instructed to stand next to me, and I was told to keep an eye on them so they didn't get out of line. I glanced over at the two residents beside me; they were grinning like Alice's Cheshire cat, too happy to be 'insiders' to cause me any trouble.

Grew struggled to straighten her jacket while still holding the heavy box of papers, juggling it from arm to arm. "Just who do you think you are? You can't just barge into my office like this!"

Frank and John reached into their pockets and flashed

their badges in unison at Grew.

Her face drained of color.

"We're the FBI," John said.

Frank pulled the warrant out from his pocket and slapped it down on the desk, "And this says we can barge into your office."

Grew's face went from white to red to purple while Frank searched the office. John kept her helpless at gunpoint.

The three bystanders, Mr. George, Mr. Jake, and me, couldn't have been happier as we watched Frank don gloves and pull out the desk drawers, methodically searching each one.

I knew what he'd find because in that desk because I'd searched those same drawers once looking for a pen.

Except he didn't find what I thought he would; he didn't pull out what I thought he would. I got the same disappointment when he rifled through the filing cabinets. He didn't keep or closely examine any of the contents of the desk or filing cabinet.

I felt defeated. If there was no evidence in her office of Grew's evil, then she may very well be able to walk away unscathed from all the chaos she'd caused in people's lives.

That's when Frank wrenched the heavy cardboard box from Grew's clutches. I thought she was going to spit in his face as he sat the box on her desk and opened it. Reaching inside he carefully pulled out some documents and laid them on the top of her polished desk.

"Well, well, well," he said, lying what I recognized as the papers printed in Chinese on the tabletop. "Billing invoices for a valium press, and several pill manufacturing tins." He examined another document. "Then you advanced to industrial multi pill press." He sat another stack of documents on top of that. "and of course any good drug business needs Fentanyl."

He stacked another row of papers on the desk. "And some binding materials to go with the Fentanyl."

He then stacked a small row of small blue folders next to

the last stack of papers. "Now, I wonder why you'd be holding the work visas for some of your foreign workers?"

"They gave them to me to hold for safe keeping!" Grew snapped at Frank.

"Yeah. I'll just bet they did. What did the ones without visas give you?"

Grew glared, but John made sure she saw the gun he held in his hand, so that's all she did.

Frank next pulled out a ledger book and flipped through it before adding it to the pile. "I'm sure you used a code to keep the names of the dealers who bought the illegal drugs from you from police detection, but the FBI has people who can crack any code easily."

He looked over at Grew, and his eyes showed pure hatred. I blanched a bit at his hard, dispassionate tone when Frank told Grew, "Janet Mulgrew you are under arrest for receiving illegal shipments from China, for the manufacture and distribution of illegal drugs, and," Frank got close to her face, and I saw her purple blanch to white, "for trafficking humans."

"You forgot suspected of murder," I added.

"Oh yeah. Suspicion of murder. too."

"This is a setup," Grew screeched. "Those documents were planted on me by Pricilla and Mark, so I'd take the rap for their drug dealings and trafficking. Pricilla started out having the residents make the pills, then she found a faster method. By the time I found out about the operation she'd had the hopper and multi-pill press setup already installed in the old laboratory."

"And that's when you killed her?" asked Frank.

"Yes. No!" Grew licked her lips and pulled on the edge of her suit jacket. "We did have an altercation, but I never strangled her. It must have been one of the drug dealers she was dealing with."

I spoke up then, "A drug dealer would not have straightened out her clothing before leaving her in the bushes."

The corner of Frank's mouth twitched up a micro-fraction. "Good point. And the finger marks on her neck were smaller, like those of a woman."

Grew defended herself by saying, "She kept asking for more money. A bigger cut. She wasn't worth it, so I had to eliminate her from the equation."

"And what did Ramon Sanchez do to cause you to try to eliminate him from the 'equation'?" asked John.

"I didn't do anything to Ramon, and now that he's dead he can't dispute that."

John looked at Frank and said, "Sanchez told me Grew and Mark forced something down his throat when they caught him in the drug manufacturing room. They thought he was dead, but he wasn't fully out when he overheard them talk about taking his dead body off somewhere so he wouldn't be found on-site. They had a lot of trouble keeping the police to just the outside of the building when they investigated Pricilla's death, and they didn't want the police coming around again to investigate and find their drug manufacturing set up.

"They left Ramon's dead body in the lab so they could go get a truck to take him and dump him far away. He managed to get outside and head for the gazebo where he knew he had a rendezvous with one of the workers."

Everyone knew I'd been the one to find Ramon. *Did they also know I was his rendezvous?* I blushed pink, but no one seemed to notice. They were all busy looking at the deep shade of purple that had returned to Grew's face.

"You're lying. The news reported that Ramon died before he could tell the police anything," Grew said.

John smiled, "We did tell the news reporters that. Seems everyone is a liar these days."

Frank picked up the top visa folder on the stack of papers. "Want to tell me the real reason you came to be holding these?"

Grew stood up tall and tugged on the edges of her jacket so hard I thought she'd pull it off.

"I told you. They gave me those for safekeeping when

they got hired. So I hired a few immigrants for cheap labor. What of it?"

"Those girls will be interviewed once we have them in a secured, safe place. Now that they are away from their handler, what do you think they'll tell us about their work conditions, their wages and the fact that you were holding their work visas?"

"I...I..." Grew snapped her mouth shut. Her face began to turn a deeper shade of purple. I feared she'd explode with rage, but then she let out a protracted breath, her shoulders rounded and she said, "I didn't know anything about any of the workers' situations. I wasn't the one to bring them on board. I had no knowledge of them."

Frank pointed to Mr. George, Mr. Jake, and me. When he spoke again, I knew why he'd let us stay in the room. "We have three witnesses to the fact that you were found leaving this office with the papers for the illegal narcotics scheme and the work visas for several immigrants, who were not paid wages and were treated as slaves while they worked for you. You have some hefty charges that can be leveled against you. You want to keep telling me you're innocent or start telling me your side of the story?"

Grew straightened up to her full height and glared at Frank. "You have no idea of how hard it is to keep this place going. I had to scrimp and save every penny. Rorry was all busted up from a drug deal gone sour when he came here to recuperate. I caught him stealing pills from Zina at night. He told me he knew the ins and outs of the drug trade and offered to help me get connections so I could make enough money to turn a profit here.

"Once I saw the going street rates for valium, and all the other street drugs, I saw the profit in selling the unused pills from the patients to a street dealer Rorry knew. That helped to keep the lights on. Only problem was, the mandatory federal narcotics forms maintained by the nurses became a problem. If they administered a pill, they logged it onto that form. If they saw a pill was missing and that form showed the pills weren't given to a resident, the nurses began to question why the pills were missing. Fortunately, they reported their concerns to me and I told them I'd take care of the situation.

"It was then I got the idea to replace the medicines we use with fakes. Most of the clients here wouldn't know the difference anyway, but I had to make sure the nurses wouldn't be any the wiser, so I ordered custom-made pill presses and the ingredients from China. The presses made the pills look enough like their real counterparts that no one noticed, but it was labor consuming to press out just one tablet at a time and I couldn't be spending my time doing that.

"I got molds to make multiple pills and hired one of the drug dealer's girlfriends to teach the residents how to make the pills at their craft time. The residents were sloppy at it, and half of what they did had to be thrown out, but at least they didn't catch on to what was going on, so no one was the wiser.

"Business was going good, so I reworked the old lab and ordered a large pill-making machine. I had the P.T. guy assemble it in the lab where we stored the outgoing drug shipments.

"Then that dammed Priscilla found out why I didn't need the residents making the pills anymore and she wanted a bigger piece of the pie. She became a problem. I didn't need her anymore since I had the pill maker machinery, so I told her she could leave—go back to servicing her drug dealer boyfriend.

"How was I to know she hated the guy and didn't want to go back? She threatened to tell the FBI about the pill making operation if I didn't let her stay on and collect a percentage of the haul. I let her stay on for a while to keep her shut up, but couldn't afford to keep splitting the proceeds with her.

"We fought. When she kept calling me a sloppy operator, I just wanted her to shut up, but she wouldn't, so I put my hands around her neck just to shut her up. Once my hands were there, I found myself choking her until she stopped breathing."

My hands flew to my throat, and a little sob escaped me

from the memory of Martin's hands on my neck.

"Priscilla's tip was the reason I started my investigation." Frank said.

"So I guess I hadn't succeeded in shutting her up?" Grew said.

"And Ramon?" Frank prompted. "What about him?"

"Several times I found Ramon talking to the girls who work the West Wing. He was a big flirt and was Latino himself, so I thought he was just trying to get laid. Then when I found him near my office on one of his breaks, I began to get suspicious. He was too friendly with the immigrants. Always asking them questions.

"I had Mark question the girls under his command. They told him Ramon had been asking them where they sleep and how they get paid. They claim they didn't tell him anything, and Mark said they were too frightened to not tell him the truth, but then I found Ramon in the North corridor, trying to break into the old laboratory. He had to go. Only I couldn't just fire him; he didn't work for me."

"He was sent here by ICE to investigate human trafficking. He must have stumbled on the drug operation by mistake," Frank explained to Mr. George, Mr. Jake and me so we could follow the story.

"Overdosing on Morphine is not a healthy way to conclude an investigation," John responded.

I spoke up then, not that I knew for sure, but I could picture the events as they must have happened. "It is true that Ramon was always propositioning the ladies, but Ramon didn't take the morphine voluntarily. Did he?" I asked Grew.

She stoned up and didn't answer.

"The morphine they gave him must have been what had been prescribed for Rorry's pain management," I said. "And I'll just bet YOU gave it to him." I pointed my finger at Grew, and knowing what would push her over the edge, I said. "You'll soon be in an orange, wrinkled jumpsuit, rotting in a filthy prison cell for his attempted murder."

"It wasn't me! Ramon took one sip of the drink I'd

prepared for him and refused to drink anymore, so Mark forced it down his throat. Mark is the one who should be brought up on attempted murder charges, not me."

CHAPTER 29

I sank down on my sofa, grateful to be back home. I still had to work to do on clearing my father's name, but I hoped that what Frank had learned, and still refused to share with me, would be of some help in that area.

I was peacefully crocheting an adorable doggie sweater for Mr M when Frank came to see me. After a brief hello kiss, I invited him in to sit with me on the sofa.

He had started growing his beard again. It made him appear rakishly handsome, but gave me worries that it was a prelude to another undercover assignment. My heart fluttered at the prospect of us having alone time and was loathe to give him up again so soon to his job.

"In all the excitement, I never got the chance to give you your Christmas present from me," Frank said.

I suddenly didn't know what to do with my hands, so I clasped them in my lap. When he pulled something from his pocket and sank down to kneel beside the sofa, I popped up, desperately terrified.

Frank's face registered confusion.

The doorbell screamed.

I raced to the door, leaving Frank behind.

He yelled out, "don't answer the door without seeing who it is first."

Milton wanted to just hand me the reports and be on his way, but I insisted he come in, meet Frank and explain the reports to me.

"These are mostly self-explanatory," Milton told me, but upon my insistence, he reluctantly entered the living room. He and Frank shook hands, and Frank relaxed a little when I explained that Milton was helping me tie up a few loose ends.

Frank frowned when Milton sat on the sofa in the spot Frank had just vacated. I sensed he was impatient for Milton to be gone so he could give me my gift, but I needed for Milton to go over those reports in laborious detail—anything to stall Frank. I had to have more time to adjust to the implications of what I suspected Frank was going to give me.

"This report shows that the pill you gave me was just sugar and some gelatin," Milton explained as he sat the laboratory test results on the coffee table while Frank paced.

"I suspected as much when Zina said the pills didn't work for her anymore and then Mrs. Jones's cat had no ill effects from eating them. I wonder what Rorry thought when he got no effect from the pills he filched from Miss Flower's nightstand?"

Frank looked at me in surprise. "How did you know Calhoun was taking Miss Flower's pills?"

"Her description of the grim reaper. Black robe and two scythes, or Rorry with his crutches."

Frank nodded and returned to his pacing.

"This report is my account of going to meet with the band member with the mandolin." Milton sat that stapled sheath of papers down.

"Did you find it?" I asked Milton.

"Yup," he told me. "This receipt is what the police gave me when I turned the Remington Vest Pistol I found in the mandolin over to them."

I picked up that receipt. "Did they tell you if the gun was the one used to kill Lana?"

Frank stopped his pacing. Staring first at Milton, then me.

Milton cleared his throat. "Not officially. They aren't supposed to share that kind of information with anyone not employed by the city anymore."

"Well?" I questioned.

Milton cleared his throat and looked at Frank, who took that moment to leave the room.

Once Milton saw he was gone, he whispered, "Yes. It was the same gun used to kill Lana."

"Oh." I felt woozy at this news.

I took the next set of documents Milton handed me. There was a picture of the bartender and the picture of me in the raincoat clipped to the report.

"The bartender at the party is really a hired killer from Kazakhstan. That was his first and last assignment with the catering firm. He's already fled the country, but the police suspect he was hired for the killing. They just don't have any idea of who hired him or why."

"I know who hired him," I said, "and I know why he had this picture and wanted to kill me."

Frank was suddenly at my side, "Kill you?" His impatience with my wanting a detailed report forgotten. Thankfully, he also forgot about giving me my Christmas present as well.

CHAPTER 30

"Yes. I took the picture of you and I paid that man to get the job as the bartender to kill you! But it was all your doing!" Guildenstein shouted at me, his face scrunched up with rage at my accusations.

I hadn't expected him to crumble so quickly. Frank was at my side, ready to protect me, but it was unnecessary. Guildenstein sank down into the chair behind his desk and put his head in his hands sobbing. "Since your aunt died, book sales for her Penelope Pembrooke mysteries have been tapering off. People are forgetting her. My finances are a mess. I'd worked a deal with your cousin because he said his sister was now part owner of the mansion and he had full access to the house. He told me he could steal the manuscripts for me. When he couldn't make good on his promises, and my debts were ballooning, I knew I had to do something."

He looked up at me, tears still streaming from his eyes. "I knew your dead husband cheated a lot of people out of their money in a Ponzi scheme and that your father was wanted for treason. If you were killed, everyone would think the murder was related to one of those criminal activities, and I'd be in the clear.

"I was planning on killing you myself. I tried on several occasions, but I always chickened out. I finagled an invitation to the party at your house. I was set on finding you and making you give me the unfinished manuscripts or finding them myself, but knew I need a backup plan. That's when I hired Boris and gave him the picture so he'd know what you looked like."

"So you hired someone to kill me? How was killing me going to help you get the manuscripts?" I asked, twirling my USB bracelet around on my wrist and without looking directly at it, making sure the decorative clasp was closed, so the bracelet's function as a digital storage device wasn't evident.

"Once you were dead, your cousins would inherit the house. Martin promised me I'd be granted full access to look for the manuscripts. I could tear the house apart if need be. What he told me sounded like a good idea. The intrigue that would surround your death would be the extra push I'd need to get those latest books to be best sellers. We could have all been rolling in the dough."

"Rolling in the dough while I rolled in my grave." I resisted the urge to take my bracelet off, throw it to the floor and stomp on it to destroy the unfinished manuscripts, but they were the last words my aunt Tilly ever wrote, and I couldn't do that.

Instead, I took a solid stance, poised my fits at my side, brought my right fist up, and—twisting my arm to rifle the blow—I struck Guildenstein full in the face.

Blood squirted from his nose, and I marveled at how I was able to watch it flow down his face without feeling faint.

My sensei was right. I just need the proper motivation to execute a perfect punch.

And Frank never raised a hand to stop me.

CHAPTER 31

Mazie sat in the sunshine of the solarium in the new residential home she'd been relocated to after the center was closed down. Her flowered print dress was as cherry as the smile on her face.

"How did you and the other residents know Grew was conducting an illegal drug manufacturing business and hiring trafficked girls?" I asked her

"We didn't. We thought Grew was stealing our food. That horrible Christmas dinner was the last straw. When I heard that helicopter coming in, I thought it was to load our food up and take it away. I had Elsie sound the alarm that it was time to riot and stop the thefts. We were darn tired of tuna noodle casserole, but that spam turkey was the last straw."

I began to laugh. "You mean Andrew's sister always saying, 'Don't drink the water' was an alarm of some sorts?"

"She was our lookout for all our planning meetings. Always let us know when someone was getting close so we could act innocent when we were caught. Her shrill voice could cut sheet metal, so she was a good choice for a lookout, but they aren't brother and sister. They're husband and wife."

"What?"

"We all kept their secret. Elsie came down with Alzheimer's, and when she started needing more care than Andrew could give, he tried to find a facility to take care of her where they could be together. As horrible as the center was, it was the most reasonably priced. Only it didn't have facilities for husbands and wives to be housed together. Fearing they'd be turned away, Andrew told the Center they were brother and sister and needed rooms close together."

"Well, well, what do you know?" I was amazed at the level of subterfuge that had gone on around me.

"So what'd they end up doing with that noisy fella Rorry?" Mazie asked me.

"He's in a federal jail awaiting charges of drug trafficking. Seems he's the one who convinced Grew there was great profit in stealing the patient's drugs. She started with taking the meds from the locked cabinets to give to him for extra money. Then she discovered she could order pill presses from China and using some common cooking ingredients, coloring agents, starch, and sugar make replicas to replace the pills she was stealing so no one would suspect the pills were gone. From there she took to making her own drugs and the business just grew, right along with her greed."

Mazie frowned. "And, the girls that didn't speak English? They were greedy Grew's idea to make more money, too?"

I hung my head in shame remembering how I shied away from Rose because I couldn't understand her when she tried to tell me things; not being able to understand her had made me uncomfortable.

"Grew got the girls from the drug dealer she was doing business with. Seems he found trafficking in humans was a more lucrative way to make money, a renewable resource of sorts with the only initial investment getting them here. If he could keep them too frightened to speak up, they wouldn't give testimony against their handlers. It seems human trafficking carries less risk of arrest then dealing in tangible things like drugs where there is obvious evidence of a crime.

"Grew gave their meager wages to their 'handler,' Mark.

Stayler. The only payment that any of the girls ever got was room and board. Mark used video surveillance of them, locked holding rooms, and the fact that most of the girls were illegals to keep them in line. They were all terrified they were going to jail, so they kept quiet."

"Tisk. Tisk. Those poor girls were slaves. What will happen to them now?"

"I don't know what will happen to the girls who were smuggled into the country in a semi, but Rose was already in the country and had a work visa when she got snared into their trafficking scheme. She gave her visa to Mark because he said he could get her a great job working in a luxury resort in Michigan, but he had to show her visa to the new employers to show she was legal to work in this country. He told her she'd be making enough money to live high on the hog and still send some home to her family in Guatemala."

Neither of us laughed at that irony.

"When she realized she'd been had, that she was working to line his and Grew's pockets, she wanted out, but he refused to give her visa back. He cooked up some phony theft charges against her and said if she went to the authorities she would be the one to go to jail and would never see or hear from her family again. Rose was terrified, but brave enough to call in anonymously to ICE."

Mazie shook her head and wiped at her eyes. "Poor Rose. And all those other girls. Working their fingers to the bone and having nothing to show for it."

"The girls have all been taken into custody, but they're refusing to talk about what happened to them," I told Mazie. "They still believe the lies they were told about going to jail and never seeing their family. Mr. Buchanan was able to get Rose to speak up and tell the truth so human trafficking charges could be filed against Grew and Mark, to go along with their other charges of murder, attempted murder, and drug trafficking."

"How'd he get Rose to cooperate?"

"Her work visa hadn't expired. All she needed to stay in

this country was a job, so Mr. Buchanan found her a job with a respectable family. She's going to be a nanny to a lovely little boy so she can stay in the United States. It's another job with room and board, but this one includes a paycheck with money to send home."

"There should be a special place in hell where they put people who prey upon the vulnerable."

"I'd consider it justice if they're consigned to experience what they've put others through."

Mazie said, "Zina and Jones are here if you'd like to say 'hi' to them."

"I sure would. Is Mrs. Jones still working on her knitting?"

"She had to start a new project. The one she was working on was turned over to the police."

"The one with the strange pattern? Whatever would they need that for?"

Mazie smiled. "It was part of our operations to find out what was happening to our food. We couldn't write down the dates and times of deliveries or the comings and goings on because the staff had access to everything and would know what we were up to, so Jones was knitting it in code, like Madame Defarge in *A Tale of Two Cities*."

Then she cleared her throat. "Enough of that. Tell me about your boyfriend the P.T. guy. I heard he was really an FBI agent. Is that true?"

"Of course not," I lied, knowing he was already on his way to Washington D. C. to testify at the arraignment hearings for Mark and Grew.

CHAPTER 32

Frank was called back to the Detroit FBI Office before he had even unpacked from his Washington D.C. trip. As disappointed as I was that we hadn't had any alone time, I was also a little relieved that I had a few more days reprieve before I had to think about dealing with my late Christmas gift from him.

I made myself a pot of hot tea, kicked off my shoes, pulled out some purple yarn, and settled on the couch to watch some "Murder She Wrote" and start working on a new sweater to replace the one I'd draped around Elsie.

Being back home felt good—until Mandy showed up.

She didn't have a key for the new locks and couldn't figure out the new-fangled alarm system that Gordon and Frank insisted be installed upon my return home, so she lay on the doorbell. Since I never had the bell reprogrammed, the doorbell screams were driving me crazy.

Seeing it was just her, I opened the door.

"So you *are* here. Just as Martin suspected." She huffed past me into the hallway.

Martin was in jail, facing conspiracy to murder charges. I'd hoped that with the house being suspected of being contaminated Mandy would stay at her high-rise apartment until his arraignment came up.

No such luck.

"So why'd you send me that phony letter saying the house was radioactive? You trying to cheat me out of my share of the house?"

"The letter didn't say the house was radioactive. It said the house was 'suspected' of being radioactive. Can I help it you panicked and left to go back to your apartment in a hurry?"

"Well, your little trick is up. I'm moving back in, and as soon as he gets out on bail, so is Martin."

"What?"

I shut off the television, threw down my yarns, ran to hide the instructions to the new security system, and ran to remove the spare house key from its spot in the kitchen.

CHAPTER 33

My heart stuttered at the sight of Frank sinking down to one knee, fishing around again in his jean's front pocket for my Christmas present. I held my breath when I caught a glimpse of something small and shiny in his hand.

I'd had days to contemplate this, but I still wasn't ready. I had the sudden urge to turn away from him and run. Run as fast and as long and as hard as I could.

"Don't do this," I told him.

"Do what?" he asked as he took my hand and kissed the back of it.

"Don't do this?" he asked as he turned my hand over and kissed the palm.

"Or this?" he asked as he dropped a ring in my open palm, stood, and kissed me where my neck and shoulder met.

A shiver took me as I closed my hand around the ring. I closed my eyes and willed my heart to stop bounding around. I squeezed the ring so hard I was afraid the diamond would cut my palm.

He kissed up my neck to the side of my face and then his lips sought my mouth. He kissed me tenderly, then waited until I opened my eyes to ask me, "Imogene Warren, you have touched my heart and have burned your way into my soul. For your sake, I tried to forget you and move on, but try as I might I can't get you out of my system. So I want to know—will you marry me?"

I squeezed my eyes shut tight again, pulled completely away from him and shook my head side to side. "You've infiltrated my heart as well and I love you more than sugar cookies; I hunger for you just as badly, but I don't see how I could possibly marry you."

I choked back a sob as I handed the ring back to him, wishing I could flee from the room, but I couldn't. My misery had me rooted right there with him.

CHAPTER 34

Frank refused to take the ring I handed to him, so I sat it on the table nearest to me.

His jaw dropped when the ring plinked down. His right hand came up and slapped his forehead, then slowly rubbed down the length of his face. His eyes began that hot, angry, smoldery look I recognized from when I first met him beside the highway hiding in his undercover car from hired killers, refusing to get out of his car or his life.

His anger melted away as quickly as it came and a look of bewilderment crossed his face as his fingers wiped the tears from my cheeks. I drew in a deep breath and found I could stop the tears if I held my breath and didn't breathe.

"I don't understand. You love me. I love you. Why wouldn't it be possible for you to marry me?" He pulled back, shoved his hands in his pockets, and began pacing back and forth in front of me, staring at the floor, no longer touching or even looking at me.

When he stopped pacing and turned to faced me again, the look of anguish on his face almost broke my heart.

I began to cry again, not able to stop the hot tears of frustration. "Don't you think I want to be able to say yes?"

"Then why don't you? You don't have any more bigamist husbands hidden anywhere do you?"

"No! I only had the one, and that was all taken care of by my attorneys. At least, I think it was."

"Even if they didn't annul the marriage, he's dead, so Jorgji can't possibly be the reason you'd tell me no," Frank said as his gaze held mine.

In some ways, Jorgji was still the reason. I kept silent because I didn't want to tell Frank that I hadn't gotten around to annulling the marriage. I didn't have the money to pay the attorney to do the work and besides, as Frank pointed out, Jorgji was dead. I mulled that over in my mind.

If Jorgji's death made me a widow, what did it matter if the marriage had been annulled or not?

Except, it did matter to me. I wanted a fresh start with Frank. Nothing hanging over us.

Was my hesitation to say yes to Frank the start of a new phobia?

"You do love me don't you?" he asked in a strained voice that broke at the end.

I looked into that face so ruggedly handsome, honest, and expectant. "With all my heart, mind, body and soul," I responded truthfully.

He exhaled a long breath. "What is it then?" He took hold of my shoulders then began kissing the tears from my face. I got some measure of control, and finally managed to stop crying, but concern still furrowed his brow. "Why are you so upset?"

"I'm terrified," I choked out in a strangled breath.

"Of me?" He let go of me and took a step back, as if I'd scorched him.

"No!" I pulled him back to me and slid my arms around him.

"Then what?" He hugged me tightly, and I smelled the fresh cotton of his shirt as I tried to find the words to explain something I had only just become aware of myself.

When I didn't answer, couldn't answer, he leaned away

from me to study my face. His eyes seared my soul, and I longed to give him the answer he sought but I couldn't. I didn't know how to put what I was feeling into words because the fear was too deeply rooted inside of me.

"I can't explain it, but the thought of getting married again is...is...terrifying." I swallowed down the bile that rose up in my throat at the thought of marriage—to anyone.

He broke into a small laugh and pulled me in tighter into his warm, strong embrace. I looked up to see the light reflected in his eyes.

He was smiling a broad smile, looking down, studying me, as his fingers stroked my wet face and jaw line. "Is that all? I've come to realize that there are things I'm terrified of, too. Things I never thought I'd be afraid of. Things I'm ashamed to admit that I'm afraid of, but there is one thing I know for sure. I know I don't want to live my life without you. When I saw you press your mouth to Ramon's beside the pond to save his life, what I felt wasn't jealousy. It was this powerful emotion of love for the person you are and a realization that I didn't want to lose you. I wanted our relationship permanent. I knew in that moment that I wanted to marry you—all the risks be damned."

He took a hold of my hand and placed the discarded ring on the ring finger of my left hand. I looked at the heart shaped diamond set in white gold and by force of will kept the bile from rising again.

Frank kissed my palm, and then stroked it lightly with his gentle fingers, sending a dozen sensations shooting through me in anticipation of sensations yet to come. "I'm just as terrified to think about what marriage means for us, for your safety, for our lives, but losing you is what terrifies me the most, more than all the other terrors combined."

"You aren't going to lose me—ever," I reassured him as I shoved aside my unfounded fears, placed my lips against his and kissed him lightly; pressing myself to him, I clung tightly to my future.

YARN GENIE DOG TOY BALL

Materials:
- Size F or G crochet hook
- Small amount of dark colored worsted weight yarn for bottom of ball.
- Small amount of light, non-white colored worsted weight yarn for top of ball.
- Small amount of white worsted weight yarn for teeth.
- Small amount of black worsted weight yarn for eyes.
- Yarn needle
- Small amount of stuffing

Abbreviations:
ch-chain
sc-single crochet
hdc-half double crochet
dc- double crochet
dc cluster-work three dc in one stitch holding back the last loop. Yarn over and draw through all loops on hook.
FO-finish off leaving long tail for sewing.

Instructions:

Bottom:
With dark color yarn ch. 2
Round 1: 6 sc in second ch from hook. Join with slip stitch to first sc. (6 sc.)
Round 2: 2 sc in each stitch around (sc increase). Join with a slip stitch to first sc. (12 sc.)
Round 3: *sc increase, sc in next stitch*, repeat from * to * around. Join with slip stitch to first sc. (18 sc)
Round 4: *sc increase, sc in next two stitches* repeat from * to * around. Join with slip stitch to first sc. (24 sc.)
Round 5: *sc increase, sc in next three stitches* repeat

from * to * around. Join with slip stitch to first sc. (30 sc.)
Round 6: *sc increase, sc in next four stitches* repeat
from * to * around. Join with slip stitch to first sc. (36 sc.)
Rounds 7 & 8: sc around. Slip stitch to first sc. FO.

Top:

Using a light color yarn work the top the same as Rounds
1-6: work the same as the bottom.
Round 7: sc in first 10 stitches. Dc cluster in next stitch.
Sc around. Join to first sc with a slip stitch.
Round 8: sc around. Join with slip stitch. FO.

Eye: (make two)

With black ch 2, work 6 sc in second chain from hook. FO
Sew eyes on either side of nose. Put a small stitch of
white yarn on the upper corner of each eye to make
them "shine." Pull all threads to the inside and secure.
No need to weave in the thread. The ends will be
covered by stuffing.

Mouth:

Attach white yarn three stitches to the right of the nose.
Sc in same stitch as attachment, hdc in next stitch, 2 dc
in next stitch, dc in next stitch, 2 dc in next stitch, hdc in
next stitch, sc in next stitch. FO.

Sew top and bottom together stuffing tightly before
completely closed.

Note: You can use one eye for a Cyclops. If yarn scraps
are used for stuffing, the ball cleans the dog's teeth
when chewed on. This is also a cute ball for kids to play
with (minus the chewing.)

ACKNOWLEDGMENTS

As with any writing endeavor, I couldn't have written this book without the help, encouragement, and input of so many people. A special thanks to the Eaton Rapids Writer and Verbosity Writing Groups where Helen Broom, Dennis Swan, Dee Cassidy, Dan Ellsworth, Lisa Dukes, Jennifer Hunnel, Katharine Scheck and Christa Scheck consistently gave me helpful feedback to refine much of the wording and plot points (and Helen kept me from feeding champagne instead of water to poor Mr. M in the laundry room).

Thank you to my friend Deb Echtinaw for supporting me at book signings and author events, and to Norma Jean Linza and Yvonne King. I sincerely appreciate your encouragement, feedback, and insight. It was that feedback that gave Imogene her next job and what allowed me to successfully place Imogene and Frank together in this third book.

A NOTE FROM THE AUTHOR

Hello. I'm glad you made it to the end of this third Yarn Genie Mystery. It was a delight to write and I hope you found it a delight to read. If you enjoyed the book, or even if you didn't enjoy the book, I would appreciate it if you would go to Amazon.com and leave a review. I do read all the reviews and try to improve my writing based on comments received. Also, reviews are critical to the success of a book and thereby the most sincere way to show an author you appreciated their work.

Every book goes through several edits to ensure an optimum reading experience. If you found an error in any of my novels, please notify the publisher at IslandCityPublishing@gmail.com. Thank you!

OTHER BOOKS BY THIS AUTHOR

Knitting Up a Murder—*Yarn Genie Mystery I*
Hooked Into Murder—*Yarn Genie Mystery II*

Made in the USA
Lexington, KY
08 June 2019